W9-BLT-010

#6053

#12.50

1/09

bird

ALSO BY RITA MURPHY

Looking for Lucy Buick

Harmony

Black Angels

Night Flying

bird

rita murphy

DELACORTE PRESS

Published by Delacorte Press
an imprint of Random House Children's Books
a division of Random House, Inc., New York

This is a work of fiction. Names, characters, places, and incidents either are the
product of the author's imagination or are used fictitiously. Any resemblance to
actual persons, living or dead, events, or locales is entirely coincidental.

Delacorte Press and colophon are registered trademarks of Random House, Inc.

www.randomhouse.com/teens
Educators and librarians, for a variety of teaching tools,
visit us at www.randomhouse.com/teachers

Library of Congress Cataloging-in-Publication Data
Murphy, Rita.
   Bird / Rita Murphy. — 1st ed.   p. cm.
   Summary: Miranda, a small, delicate girl easily carried off by the wind, lands at
Bourne Manor on the coast of Lake Champlain and is raised by the dour Wysteria
Barrows, but she begins to believe rumors that the Manor is cursed and, aided by a
new friend and kites secreted in an attic, seeks to escape.
   ISBN 978-0-385-73018-1 (hardcover)—ISBN 978-0-385-90557-2
(hardcover lib. bdg.)
   [1. Dwellings—Fiction. 2. Supernatural—Fiction. 3. Flight—Fiction. 4. Kites—
Fiction. 5. Foundlings—Fiction. 6. Champlain, Lake—History—19th century—
Fiction. 7. Vermont—History—19th century—Fiction.]   I.Title.
   PZ7.M9549Bir 2008   [Fic]—dc22   2008004690

The text of this book is set in 11.75-point Adobe Caslon.
Book design by Vikki Sheatsley
Printed in the United States of America
10 9 8 7 6 5 4 3 2 1
First Edition

To my loving family

1

Wysteria did not care where I had come from or where I had been. Nor did she care that I was small and delicate in nature and easily carried off by the wind. She cared only that I stay with her in the great house she occupied on the eastern shore of Lake Champlain.

I came to Bourne Manor on a bright morning in the month of February just as the winter snows had settled in for good along the shore, taking up residence in the open fields and across the cliffs. In those days, I was often picked up by the wind and left in odd places because of it—blown into the tops of low trees or caught up in the scrubs or briars—though never before had I been taken so close to the turbulent waters of a lake.

Knocked hard by a gust, left tangled in the branches of one of the lone elms that skirted the bay, I remembered little of what had come before; only a series of faceless relatives and small drafty houses; only a hollow feeling of something that had once been but was no longer.

From that lonely elm, I was retrieved by two of Wysteria's Hounds. Pulled from the branches by their strong jaws. I was lost and Wysteria found me. Or perhaps the Manor itself found me, beckoning me to its gates on that February morning.

The home of Wysteria Barrows was a looming structure that had the appearance of having grown sideways out of the earth. Though firmly anchored, it listed dramatically to the left like an old tree turned by the wind, its foundation clinging to the red stone cliffs for support as a tern might cling in a storm.

The Manor was four stories in height with three turrets, two balconies and a widow's walk at its pinnacle. Its once-ivory paint had been stripped by rough weather, returning it to its natural gray clapboard, and Wysteria had left it so. There were twenty-two rooms in the Manor, five staircases, ten fireplaces and one slender tower on the west wing that held my room, a room with vaulted ceilings and windows that looked out over the harbor and across to the wild Adirondack Mountains. A grand place, my room. And indeed Bourne Manor itself was grand. No grander house could you find in the islands or on the mainland.

As grand as the Manor was, it was always a lonely place, destined from its beginning to be set apart from all other houses. Some said the Manor harbored an ill-gotten fortune within its walls, which carried a terrible and irreversible curse. Others believed that its foundation stones, having been laid crooked, forever doomed it to a perverse and tragic end. Whichever story was true, Bourne Manor knew little happiness within its walls. The four generations of grim ancestral portraits lining the main stairwell bore testimony to this, as did the vacant and lifeless rooms that towered over the cliffs.

The Manor's ballroom had never been used for dancing, as far as I knew, nor the parlors for entertaining guests, for no guests ever came there. To those on the outside, it was a strange and mournful dwelling that made for ghost stories, of which there were many and for good cause. For although no one ever perished unnaturally within its walls that I knew of, the Manor, set out on its own as it was, battered by the wind, invited the spirits of those long departed and of those who roamed the shores in search of a warm fire, as it had invited me. The lost and aimless: to these Bourne Manor gave its shelter.

2

I was adept from an early age at the art of spinning and making lace. Wysteria, seeing my natural ability to weave, instructed me in the crafting of nets. My slender fingers took easily to this trade, slipping freely through the tenuous holes and seams. Running shuttles and threading meshes came as naturally to me as breathing, and I caught on quickly to the work at hand.

Mending nets for the fishing fleet out of St. Albans was how Wysteria made her living, how she fueled the giant coal furnace in the depths of the Manor, how she kept food in the pantry. With my nimble fingers to weave for her, with my strong eyes to see and tie the knots, Wysteria was free to spend her time with the figures and sums, bargaining with the fleet owners over the best price for our work.

I became an invaluable asset to Wysteria, and I see now that she never would have let me go even if someone had come looking, and perhaps they had. Perhaps a tall man with eyes the same color as mine had come rapping on the front door early one morning, inquiring about a little girl who had been taken from him by the wind. Wysteria would have shaken her head, offered her condolences and sent him away. The Manor was everything to her, and as I could remember no other life, it became everything to me as well. I was warm and well fed, and when a person has known hunger, when she has spent a night in the brambles and awoken to a gray sky with no hope of heat or warmth, small but essential comforts bind her to her keeper.

Whether anyone came to the Manor in search of me, I will never know, but I did occasionally see others as Wysteria and I ventured, as a matter of necessity, to the nearby town of Georgia Plains, a small cluster of buildings and storefronts five miles' walk from the Manor. We were a most unusual couple: she tall and willowy, with a dramatic nest of white hair piled on top of her head, and I small, my gait slowed by the heavy steel-weighted boots she had made for me.

In those early years, when I was still allowed outside the Manor, Wysteria had fashioned, with the help of the local shoemaker, a pair of boots with a steel plate in each sole to keep me anchored to the ground. She insisted I wear them always, as she feared above all else that I would be carried off by another random gust and lost to her forever.

The open fields and pastures surrounding the Manor were prone to strong blasts off the lake, so whenever we went out we kept to the railroad bed, which was sheltered by a stand of tall pines. There were as well fewer eyes upon us along the rails than on the main road, for as you can imagine, we were a source of much interest in those days. My presence at the Manor, in particular, was a matter of ample gossip in town, as was my diminutive size. This was not helped by the appearance of my clothing, a mix of styles and Wysteria's unique ability with a needle and thread. My petticoats and skirts were constructed from her many silk evening gowns, lace-edged at the hem and neck. In between, the heavy wool of a fisherman's peacoat covered my bodice and arms. There was no shortage of wool in the trunks that graced the foyers and stairwells of Bourne Manor. It made up the foundation of most of my outfits.

"Wool deflects water," Wysteria insisted, unfolding yards of it on to the clothesline to air. "It breathes and keeps the soul warm."

"It's itchy," I complained. But Wysteria did not give my grievance a moment's thought, in the same way that she did not concern herself with the gossip of the locals, as she referred to them. She never addressed any by name, though I'm sure she must have known their names. The locals were merely there to supply her with small necessities and occasional expertise in the repair of the Manor. Beyond this, she gave little thought to whom or what they chose to talk about. She felt herself far above the common person, though she had started out poorer than most and had only married well, inheriting Bourne Manor from her late husband, Captain Lawrence Barrows, a quiet, reserved gentleman who had had a successful career at sea. It was rumored that Wysteria had married the captain solely for his fortune, that she had never loved him. And, to his great sorrow, refused to bear him any children.

When the captain drowned in the lake during a spring storm, it was no loss to Wysteria. She simply settled his accounts, closed off his study on the third floor and went forward with the upkeep of her one remaining asset, the one thing that kept her above the locals and far from the dirty fishing shacks out on the pier.

"Miranda." This was the name Wysteria had

chosen for me. I'm not sure where she found it. Perhaps it had belonged to another or been borrowed from the pages of a book. Perhaps she simply liked the way it flowed smoothly from the tongue. She said it fit me, though I could not see that myself.

I remembered once that someone had called me Peege and once Meg. Concise, one-syllable names—easy to remember. When you are as small as I was, people often shorten your name, along with their esteem of you, in proportion to your size. Peege could easily disappear. Meg could stand in the shadows. Miranda was needed. Perhaps that is why I stayed longer than I should have with Wysteria. I believed she needed me.

"Miranda, must you drag your feet so? Are they so heavy that you cannot bear to walk like a proper lady?" The boots weighed as much as I did. More, perhaps. I hated them. They may have kept me from the wind, but they were cumbersome and ungraceful and took all my energy to shuffle about in. To reach Georgia Plains was a difficult chore, and I often wished, upon our arrival, to lie down and rest on one of the benches in the town square, but Wysteria would never allow such a thing. We were the owners and residents of Bourne Manor, and as such, we were to remain dignified at all times and never to show signs of fatigue or weakness.

"I will try harder, Wysteria."

"See that you do."

I picked up my weary feet and followed her into the shops.

I did not know any of the shopkeepers or the children. Wysteria felt that with my physical delicacy, school was an unnecessary burden she'd rather not subject me to, and so took on the task of educating me in her own unique way.

We studied everything Wysteria was interested in and no more. I learned to figure and do my sums, as Wysteria loved money above all else. She kept it hidden in various places about the Manor. She counted it, stacked it and doled it out in miserly sums. She taught me how to keep the accounts and frequently tested my memory on the names of all the prominent fishing captains along the lake. I learned from Wysteria the geography of Vermont and Fairfax County, and everything there was to know about dogs, particularly wolfhounds, of which she had four. These beasts had no names of their own. Wysteria did not believe in such things. We simply referred to them as the Hounds, which worked well, as they all looked exactly alike and you never saw one without the others. I was often given the task of feeding the Hounds and combing them out after they spent the day roaming the fields, collecting burrs from their shaggy gray fur. The Hounds were bigger than I was, and I had a strange and perhaps unnatural fear of them. I was quite sure they would suddenly turn and ravage me, eat me up entirely. The Hounds, however, were my charges, and I had to learn to face them and, to some degree, trust them. They growled on occasion, exposing their gums and sharp teeth, but in general they were content to lie at my feet while I wove and did my lessons.

I wished that Wysteria had told me about the history of Bourne Manor, about the wind and the currents, and something of the lake tides, but these were not topics she wished to discuss, and so I did not learn them until much later. But I did not mind studying at home. The village school, a cramped clapboard house on the edge of town, would have been much worse. Going there would have meant facing the daily walk along the rails and the stares of the local people, for it was clear from the beginning that I was not welcome among them, not only because of my size, but also because of my relationship to the Manor.

"The heir of Bourne Manor," the ladies in the shops would murmur as we passed through. I heard the phrase spoken by the men in the fish market and whispered through the spokes of the children's

bicycle wheels. That I was the Bourne heir meant little to me, and rightly so, for there was no inheritance
or legacy waiting for me beyond the old house itself,
despite what some thought. The Manor's only value
came from the secret that lay within it.

3

The attic of Bourne Manor was filled with all manner of strange inventions. The day I finally found my way inside, I thought the room full of savage birds. Great gossamer wings and sharp beaks met me; exotic tails encircled my head. I screamed and turned away, fearing I would be picked up at any moment by their fierce talons.

But they were, of course, not birds, for what birds can live in a cage, even one of that size, for long? They were kites. Dozens of silk and paper kites intertwined with laces and strings and arched bamboo frameworks. Their designs were foreign to me, wild swirls and pinwheels of color, painted faces and bared teeth. They were tied at the ends with fanciful ribbons and feathers, and all the paper kites, every single one, trailed braided cords and oddly shaped clasps.

How I found this extraordinary room and came to mingle with the great wings was a mystery in itself, for it was not a place that was meant to be found, as there was never a more arduous task in finding anything.

Every room in the Manor, with the exception of the widow's walk and the enormous open sitting room on the first floor, was locked. There was a key for every door and also for every cupboard and every drawer of every desk. There was even a key to lock and unlock the windows. Every evening at ten o'clock Wysteria walked the halls of the Manor locking each door, including my own, and then unlocking them again at dawn. She carried all the keys on a great chain kept at her waist, and only she knew which key was which.

"I lock the rooms, Miranda," she explained, "to keep out the drafts. I cannot bear a draft, not even of the smallest kind." She spoke as if a lock could keep the wind from slipping under the doors or stealing across the floorboards. Obsessed with drafts, Wysteria was forever stuffing bits of old newspaper into cracks in the walls. It made little sense to me, but I never questioned her in the beginning. I trusted her then more than I trusted myself, and I honestly did not care to go into any of the dark and vacant rooms. Better that they stay locked, I thought, and keep whatever was inside, draft or not, away from me in the night. But as I grew older and spent more and more of my days inside, the lure of the upper floors of the Manor conquered my imagination and I began to wonder what lingered behind the locked doors. What was it that Wysteria tried to hold in or keep out? I wondered. Perhaps, as some believed, the rooms were filled with a rare fortune and stacked from floor to ceiling with gold coins, or perhaps they held only dusty and useless furniture, the remnants of a time long past. I found myself watching her carefully when she chose a key, waiting for my opportunity to examine it more closely. But Wysteria never let the keys leave her side; even when she walked into town, she carried them on her person.

Wysteria left many nets for me to mend whenever she went out of the Manor, secure in the notion that I would spend my hours quietly consumed with my weaving and have the repairs complete upon her return.

One afternoon in late October, before Wysteria departed for town, she presented me with a heavy load of nets. "Will twenty keep you, Miranda?"

"Yes. Twenty will do." Twenty nets required several hours of tedious attention on my part, for many of them concealed rusted hooks which could lodge easily in my palms. It was treacherous work, and though I was careful never to get caught on a barb, my fingers were often left raw and bleeding after many hours of pulling against the rough cordage.

It did little good to complain to Wysteria, for she believed that the only cure for bleeding fingers was more work. "Building up proper calluses is the only solution, Miranda. More nets is the answer to your suffering." Wysteria always seemed pleased at the sight of my tortured skin, as if it showed a serious commitment to my work. Whether or not I believed that callused skin was a sign of a job well done, I was never able to harden my own against the rubbing of the nets.

"Perhaps I will bring you a gift from town," Wysteria offered upon leaving. She did not spend money on gifts in the usual sense. She never brought a doll or a new dress home to reward me for my work. My reward, she reminded me, was a sound roof over my head and food on the table. To purchase a small tin of candies or a sachet for my drawer was extravagant on her part.

"Thank you, Wysteria. That would be fine."

The Hounds rose from beside the fire in anticipation of Wysteria's departure, and I rose with them to see her off.

"I shall return no later than six o'clock. Tend the fire and mend the nets. If I'm not back by nightfall, light the lantern." I assured her I would. Lighting the lantern was, by far, my favorite part of the day.

Perched at the very top of the Manor, encircled by the widow's walk, was a little house made entirely of glass. It was reached by a trapdoor, which opened up into a spacious room. At the very center of this room stood a table with an enormous lantern upon it. Each night after supper, I lit the lantern, as every caretaker of Bourne Manor had done since the house was built. The closest light was twenty miles to the north at Bolton Island, and so, in the event of fog, Bourne Manor kept a lantern burning midlake for any ship coming in late off the water and to warn all souls against sailing too close to the rocks that guarded its shores.

The central chimney of the Manor passed through the glass house, and its opening could be reached from the roof. It was situated as such for access in the event of fire. Three large bags of sand sat at the ready to be poured into the flue to prevent the whole structure from burning to the ground. Fire from either the lantern or the chimney was Wysteria's greatest fear, and she instructed me early on never to put wet logs in the grate or leave the lantern case open, for often we used lamp oil instead of candles and oil was most flammable.

Outside the glass house was the actual walk itself, surrounded by a wrought-iron railing, where wives supposedly paced while waiting for their husbands to return from the sea. You can be sure that there were no recent grooves of worried soles marking the walk of Bourne Manor, as Wysteria had never waited up for her husband when he was alive. The only signs of activity were the faded and ancient markings of the heels of previous Barrows women, barely covered over by the scrapes from my own steel-weighted boots when I braved the wind and walked it myself.

I loved coming up into that glass house at night on a full moon with the stars, when they were visible, just out of reach. Walking out into the sky or off the precipice of a mountain could have provided no better view. The quiet, the darkness, the sweet sulfur of the match being struck, the running of the wax, were close to heaven, as close to heaven as I had ever been.

From that height, everything seemed possible, and the oppressive and mournful nature of the house fell away from me.

Whenever Wysteria left the Manor, I'd run directly to the top floor and burst onto the walk to catch a parting glimpse of her long, dark cape bustling down the road with the Hounds in close pursuit. In her younger years, she had often traveled to Boston and New York, but of late she ventured no farther than Georgia Plains or the city of Burlington, thirty miles to the south. Still, her departure guaranteed me hours alone to do as I pleased, to spend my day at the top of the house if I so desired, to look down on the life below me and imagine myself free.

That October afternoon, Wysteria's thin figure having just disappeared around the bend, I settled myself on the large trunk that served as a bench in the glass house. I often brought the nets up there with me—the light was better than down by the fire—but that day I had left them in the foyer, still tangled and snarled, wet from the boats. I was in no hurry to make sense of them yet. They could wait.

The day was clear and cloudless. The sun had risen early, warming the glass on the windows and dancing off the swells on the lake. Though it was warm inside, a chill still hung in the air, and so I opened the trunk on which I was sitting to pull out a wool blanket for my shoulders. I shook it vigorously to knock out the dust, and when I did, a key fell to the floor. It was long and thin with unusual engravings upon it, and from its shape I could tell that it was no ordinary key but a skeleton key, a key that could open more than one door, possibly all. I returned the blanket to the trunk, immediately descended the ladder and diligently began trying the key in every lock in the Manor. By late afternoon, I'd found that it opened all the rooms on the third floor, including my own. After all my years of curiosity, I was greatly disappointed to discover that the rooms were nothing more than dim and barren chambers. There was no hidden fortune, no ancient furniture that seemed worthy of a lock.

The only room that was not empty was Captain Barrows's study, a large, handsome chamber with a broad stone hearth and bay windows looking out over the water. A sturdy rolltop desk stood in one corner, and heavy woven rugs covered the floor. With the exception of a thick layer of dust from lack of use, the study was surprisingly comfortable. The other rooms were cold and sparsely furnished in comparison, not places where I wished to spend any time. The captain's study, on the other hand, was warm and full of his life.

Wysteria never spoke of her husband, but that winter, as I spent every free moment I could in his study, I came to know Captain Lawrence Barrows, and I began to like this man whom I had never met, and never would. I came to know him only through his model ships, the logs of his days at sea and the many maps that marked his journeys. The captain had sailed around the world twice, had frequented castles and dined with thieves. And he had the great generosity to help one small girl find her way, for it was from the captain's room, through a hidden passage, that I discovered the entrance to the attic and his bevy of kites.

4

Each morning, before the sun rose and while Wysteria still slept, I used the skeleton key to leave my bedchamber and make my way to the attic and then to the widow's walk to fly the captain's kites.

I had come upon the entrance to the attic purely by chance, having accidentally fallen against the far wall of the captain's study as I tried to free a volume from his bookcase. My weight was enough to move the wall ever so slightly, allowing me to see that it was in fact not a wall at all but a slender panel that when pushed open revealed a steep and narrow staircase. At the top of the stairs was a door that could not be opened by any key, and so I spent several fretful hours picking at it with a hairpin and file. Once inside, I was quickly overtaken by its curious contents: dozens of kites, a few bolts of silk and what appeared to be a paper-making device equipped with screens, frames and buckets for mixing slurry. After more than an hour's examination, I took several kites from their shadowy lair up onto the walk to examine them in the light, for there was also a stairway that led from the attic, through a hatch that blended perfectly with the floorboards of the glass house.

As far as Wysteria knew, I entered the walk only by the obvious trapdoor and only in the evenings to light the lantern. I had no business up there at any other time, and she would have been shocked and angered to find me there with the captain's kites about me, for I suspected she knew nothing of their existence. Yet I could think of no place I would rather be. In the light of day, the walk was most spectacular.

From the top of the house, I could see all of Fairfax County, and absolutely no one could see me. Only a rare gull flying inland might catch a sideways glimpse as I stepped outside onto the walk and let my hair loose. Long and wild and set free of its braid, it was whipped about me in all directions by the strong breezes. In Wysteria's presence, I was required to keep it securely fastened and pulled tight to my head, as she did her own. "A woman's hair is a vanity of the worst kind, Miranda," she often preached at the dinner table.

Although no portrait of her hung on any of the Manor's walls, it was evident that Wysteria valued her looks and harbored her own unique brand of vanity. I often observed her admiring her reflection in the mirror above the stone mantel in the sitting room. That Wysteria had once been attractive was not difficult to imagine. She had distinctly fine features, high cheekbones and translucent porcelain skin. Her figure was still as slender as a young woman's. It was not surprising that she clung to her looks; after all, they had saved her from a life of poverty. Yet we were never to speak of appearances. If one was good-looking, one did not mention it. Beauty spoke for itself.

Try as I might, I could not see Wysteria as truly beautiful, for she possessed a cold, hardened quality. I certainly could not see her hair set free and roaming down her shoulders.

I loved the way my own hair fell into the breeze, though, and I would stand, a little too long perhaps, imagining what it would be like to let not only my hair but my whole self be taken again by the wind. Not since the day I was blown to Bourne Manor had I felt the awesome and frightening sensation of that powerful current sweeping beneath my feet, the strange invisible hands pushing me forward faster than I could go myself. I remembered distinctly that familiar prodding at my back, the brush of air at my side and the sudden feeling of being cut loose from the earth and carried along like a leaf. There was nothing I could do, no stopping it.

"Not so high," I'd called out that last time. "Not so high!" But the wind had done as it pleased, tossing and lifting my light frame into the currents.

Though I cannot remember anyone ever seeing me taken up, there was always the lingering feeling upon landing or finally getting caught by a branch that perhaps someone had seen and, finding no rational explanation for what they'd witnessed, would judge me strange and maybe even wicked in some way. I knew that my being taken by the wind was something that must never be mentioned, something that must always be held close.

Perhaps one day the wind would come for me again, but until then I felt its power in the captain's kites, which over time I smuggled up to the glass house on my evening's watch and kept hidden inside the large trunk. My favorite was the Red Dragon. I'd named it for its fierce face and vibrant color. There were many kites with bold faces and long, swift tails, but the Red Dragon was different from the others. It was the most delicate of all, with silk so finely layered it resembled the wings of a dragonfly. It was, too, the most spirited, wild and impetuous like a young bird, ardently pulling against its line and diving dangerously close to the Manor.

I could not take the chance that Wysteria might ever see a kite flying from the top of the house, so I always flew the Red Dragon on the lake side, far from her window and far from the branches of the great elm tree. I was more likely to be swept away at that high spot with a kite in my hand than down at the shoreline, and, not wanting to end up pasted to the outside of Wysteria's bedroom window, I took the precaution of securing myself to the wrought-iron railing with a long anchor line I'd rescued the summer before from the tide. It smelled of milfoil and fish gone rancid, and I hated to wrap it around myself, for I knew the rank odor would seep into the fibers of my wool bodice, requiring me to wash and dry it so as not to arouse Wysteria's suspicion. The line remained a necessity, however, as I had stayed as small and thin as on the day that I'd arrived, though I was no longer as frail as in those early years.

I was never sure exactly how the captain's kites were meant to be flown. The silk kites were simple enough, but the paper kites were unlike anything I had ever seen, as if a part of each was missing or was meant to be connected to something greater than itself. How to explain the extra cords and clasps that hung from their frames? How to decipher the meaning of the little flaps wrapped tightly to the midpole of each?

I could not cast the kites into the air with a running start, as one would on the beach, but instead had to fly them from a standing position on the walk. I devised a system of slowly letting out the line while holding a kite as far as I could from myself, setting it free only when I sensed enough of a breeze picking it from the underside and puffing it gently away from me. Of course, there were days, particularly in the fall and spring, when the weather was too wild to fly any of the kites, even the more robust paper ones, and I kept them inside. I felt a strong obligation to the captain's creations and didn't wish any to come to harm.

I became an expert in charting the weather, searching offshore for signs of low-lying clouds or fog and spotting thunderheads. I could feel the wind calling to me on certain days in those wild clouds, and I knew that given a chance it would come for me, ripping at the layers of the heavy woolen dresses and overcoats that Wysteria had so carefully stitched, and steal me away, leaving me high in a tree, or on the top of one of the mountains across the lake. I was not yet ready for such a journey. For that kind of journey I needed time. I needed Farley.

5

In the seventh year that I lived with Wysteria Barrows, my isolation came to an end. For that spring, as the forsythia bloomed on the cliffs and the sea grass took root, I met the boy named Farley.

There are certain people who glide so swiftly and immediately into your life that their entrance is almost invisible. I cannot say whether it was morning or afternoon when I first spotted Farley, with his distinctive red wool cap, wandering the shoreline, only that it was spring, as that is the season I most associate with him. Spring and the smell of lilacs.

That year, spring followed a long, hard winter, and the nets Wysteria brought home for me were in desperate shape, having been torn on the ice and snagged by driftwood. It was rare that I had a day to leave them or to be away from Wysteria, as she had a tendency to hover when there was little money and much work to be done, which was the case that year. As well, the bitter winter had left her with a lingering cough, rendering her thin and weak and more in need of me than usual. I had taken over the upkeep of the accounts while she recovered, and was painfully aware of the little we had left.

"One hundred nets this week, Miranda, and not one less. The cupboards are in a pitiful state." My fingers ached at the prospect.

The winter supply of wheat and oats Wysteria and I had stored away in October was almost gone. There was no sugar or butter, and the salt cod we often took as payment for our work was running low. We resisted combing the beach to uncover mussels so early in the season, but we often resorted to pulling long, slimy ropes of kelp from the bay and boiling them into a soup. It was full of sand and tasted of rotten fish, but it filled our stomachs while we waited.

"Why must it always come down to the wire?" Wysteria complained one morning as we ate the last bit of bread in the pantry the day before Captain Stewart made payment.

It did seem that no matter how much work we took in, the month of April was always lean. "Time to clean out the blood," Wysteria generally offered in response to our yearly dilemma and the grim condition of the pantry. "Fast hard and true before the bounty of summer takes hold." But her tone was not as staunch that year. A sound bowl of meat broth would have done us both good.

Through the blizzards and frozen nights of late February and early March, we'd had enough to eat, and the furnace had blown out its share of warmth. We'd closed off most of the Manor and kept company in the great room on the first floor in front of the massive stone fireplace. We'd even slept there on occasion, bundled in quilts and woolen blankets, our hats pulled down over our ears. On milder days, when I wasn't keeping track of the Hounds, I spent my time in the captain's study repairing the kites, replacing ragged tails with new ones and gingerly pasting the fine paper panels around their slender frames where they had broken free.

With the good weather now upon us, I longed to escape from Wysteria's presence and the damp and gloom of the Manor. If I had waited for her to leave the fireside, I might well have waited into the summer, so I took the chance of stealing away to the walk one afternoon while she napped.

The breeze that day was warm and mild, and I did

not bother to tie myself to the railing but instead slipped on my heavy boots and launched the Red Dragon.

The wind took it easily up and out past the elm to the dunes at the far end of the beach. It was a glorious sight. Its rich color was set off by the deep blue of the sky. It had better balance now with the new tail I had made for it, an array of thin silk ribbons that raced playfully behind, giving the Dragon a whimsical appearance.

When it had reached a height of more than twenty feet, I tied it off on the railing and bent down to adjust the laces of my boots. They were long laces, forever breaking free of the stays that held them in place, and had to be retied countless times in the course of a day. The shoemaker's design lacked one important feature: a button to string the laces around at the top. I had tried sewing buttons on myself, but none of the needles in Wysteria's mending basket were stout enough to pierce leather. Through the years, I had found that wrapping the laces firmly about my ankle several times and knotting them twice could keep them in place.

I carefully tucked the remaining cordage inside the top of each boot to keep it from straying and stood up slowly, instinctively reaching for the tether of the Dragon, but it was not there. It had loosened itself and wandered to the far side of the rail. I made a futile lunge for the end of the line, sure that I could retrieve it and pull it back in, but it eluded my grasp and drifted away. I was stunned. I had never lost hold of a kite. I was always steadfast in my duty of keeping them within range and could not believe my eyes as the tether disappeared over the railing's edge. All I could do was watch as the Dragon rose, then dipped dramatically to the east, its exotic tail fluttering behind.

Unaccustomed to its freedom, it wandered, at first high above the bay and then scouring along the sand. If I had not been so afraid of losing it forever, I would have appreciated the beauty of its dance. Nothing holding it back, it soared in a way not possible when attached to a harness, rising and dipping and finally disappearing around the cliff's edge. I did not see it reappear and so determined that it must have caught itself on a rock or crashed in the sand just beyond the cliffs. It would have been a walk of no more than ten minutes to find and retrieve the Dragon from its snare, but I could not simply stroll out the front door and rescue it as an ordinary person might. Wysteria was at home and would know if I left. She would hear the click of the latch on the front door, a sound I had not made since the day of the storm almost one year before.

I had on that particular morning left the Manor to walk unaccompanied to the shore to collect seaweed. I'd laced on my boots and taken one of the heavy mesh sacks that hung by the door. The Hounds had stayed behind, occupied with a ball of rough twine they had uncovered in the brush. I'd become bold, wandering farther and farther from the Manor, safe in the knowledge that the steel plates in my boots would keep me anchored to the earth. Wysteria had allowed this outing, as I was more help to her if I could fetch and carry, though she would never send me all the way into town on my own.

Whether it was the result of the storm beginning to blow in off the lake or of my desire to walk close to the cliff's edge that afternoon, I cannot say, but on my return, my sack heavy with wet kelp, I was thrust suddenly and violently off the cliff and onto the beach below. As though a giant's hand had smacked me to the earth, I was pinned with my face pressed hard into the sand. No sooner had I recovered than I was lifted and hurled into a hawthorn bush, where Wysteria later found me.

After that day, and several tedious and futile attempts to create heavier and safer boots, I was forbidden ever to leave the Manor without Wysteria by my side.

"You are, as I have always surmised, overly susceptible to the wind, Miranda, and I cannot afford to have you flying off from me or injuring yourself beyond repair. From now on, it is the safety of the fireside for you."

In the months that followed, I often asked to go outside on my own, if only for brief excursions, but my requests were adamantly denied. Wysteria had not forgotten my narrow escape, nor would she ever forget, and she reminded me resolutely that I could not control myself when it came to the weather and therefore must be protected for my own good.

"One day, Miranda, when you have attained your full weight and stature, you may perhaps once again venture forth into the world unaccompanied, but not until then" was the only consolation Wysteria offered me.

I followed her mandate, not only because there was no other choice, but also because I had begun to fear the wind as she did. Fear is a strange thing. It can creep quite unnoticed into your mind, seize hold of your reason and take root. Gradually, I grew accustomed to Wysteria's distinct brand of fear, taking it upon myself like an extra layer of wool. Until the day the Dragon broke free, I had forgotten that it was possible to live any other way.

As I stood on the walk, watching for any sign of the kite, my eyes caught hold of a small dot moving rapidly along the beach. There were times when an otter from the creek would lose its way and head along the shore. I had watched several amble about in search of food and familiar smells, avoiding the seabirds. The gulls ruled that piece of sand and had a tendency to dive at any creature that did not belong. This dot, however, was no otter, unless otters could stand and run on two legs. I wished that I had had the captain's spyglass with me to see in more detail, but I had only my own eyes. With considerable squinting, I made out the figure of a boy in a red cap. I could tell he was a boy not because of the length of his hair, for it was wild and unkempt and curled from under his cap like an ocean's wave, but because of the exuberance with which he ran. In town, the boys ran farther and faster and wilder than any girl ever did. They never seemed to care whether their clothes got soiled or their pants torn. I envied them this and had secretly decided that if I had any say in the matter, I would like to come back in my next life as a boy and spend my days at sea.

From the widow's walk, all sounds were merely

echoes by the time they reached my ears. I could never have heard him, even if the wind had been blowing to the east, but I could tell that he was yelling something as he ran in the direction of the downed kite. He vanished around the bend and quickly reappeared, holding it triumphantly over his head so that I could see. I waved at him, excited that the Dragon, except for the loss of its tail, looked intact.

So thrilled was I at its rescue that the sound of the bell was almost inaudible. Wysteria had taken to keeping a bell at her side to summon me from my room, where she assumed I spent my time. At the sound of the bell, I was to drop whatever I was doing and make her tea, or fetch another blanket for her lap, or commence some tedious chore she had devised for me. I waved to the boy and sadly left the walk, sliding swiftly down the ladder.

All during lunch—for that was the reason Wysteria had called me—I wondered about the boy, where he'd come from and what he intended to do with the Dragon. If he was a typical boy, like the ones in the village, with their slingshots and marbles, he would no doubt run home with it, not knowing what he carried in his hands. He would take it apart to see how it worked and put it back together again, forgetting some important piece. He'd fly it until it was broken and full of holes and no longer of use to anyone and then abandon it to the garbage heap. If I hadn't been so careless, I would still have had the kite in my possession.

"Miranda, this soup is too salty. Whatever have you put into it?"

"Nothing, Wysteria. It is the same as always."

At that moment, the Hounds suddenly stood up and began to growl and I returned to the kitchen to try the soup myself. It was no saltier than any other soup I had made, but I added another cup of water just the same.

"I will do better next time," I said, bringing out a new bowl and placing it on the table beside her.

"Never mind," she sighed. "It will have to do." The Hounds continued growling.

"Get ahold of yourselves!" Wysteria scolded them. They whimpered, standing rigid with attention, their noses pointing toward the front entrance. There was a faint scuffling sound outside, followed by a firm knock. The Hounds went wild, baying and running about in circles. I noticed a shadow descend over Wysteria's ashen face. I started toward the door, but she snapped her fingers at me.

"I will answer it." She stood slowly, wrapping her

shawl about her thin shoulders, and, with considerable effort, walked toward the giant oaken door, grasped the handle and pulled it open. The Hounds made a dash for freedom. They were not guard dogs by nature, and after running around the visitor a few times, realizing that he did not fear them and had not come bearing food, they lost interest and bounded off.

On the threshold stood the boy with the red cap, holding the Dragon at his side. He was thin and wiry, with a splash of freckles across his nose, and wild, curly black hair. From his stance and apparent lack of trepidation at the sight of Wysteria and the Hounds, I could tell that he knew nothing about us.

He swept off his cap. "Good afternoon, mum," he said, a slight accent gracing his speech.

"I found this on the beach." He proudly held up the Dragon in one hand and its tail in the other.

"That is fortunate for you, young man, but I fail to see how that has anything to do with me." Wysteria's tone was sharp, and I flinched as I always did at the acidity of her words, but the boy did not hesitate.

"Not you," he said. "The girl. The pretty one, with the long, dark hair." I peered out from behind Wysteria. "Her," he said, pointing to me. "The kite is for her."

"Miranda?" Wysteria turned to me. Her eyes narrowed. She seemed perturbed, not only by the boy's intrusion, but also by the reference to my hair and my being pretty, for of course we never spoke of such things. Fortunately, I could see that she had no interest in kites or knowledge of her husband's creation.

"I know nothing of it," I said calmly, surprising even myself. She turned back to the boy and I smiled widely and gave him a nod.

"There, you see, young man. We know nothing about the owner of your kite. We are very busy here and must get on with our work. Please do not intrude upon our solitude again."

"Oh," the boy said, clearly puzzled. " 'Tis a grand kite." His voice rose in admiration at the end of the sentence, and I knew that he must be from far away, perhaps another country entirely, though, never having been anywhere, I had no idea where that could be. "I'll return it to its owner when I find her," he said, putting his cap back on and tipping it at me.

Wysteria closed the door abruptly, without bidding him good day. "Bothersome," she mumbled, coughing into her handkerchief. "How dare he walk up here with no warning, no introduction! Doesn't he know who we are?"

"Apparently not, or he wouldn't have come," I

said, only meaning to state the obvious, but Wysteria took it as impertinence and glared at me.

"Why do you think he came *here*, Miranda?"

"I have no idea. Perhaps it is because we are the only house along this stretch of beach."

"Perhaps," Wysteria said, though she seemed to doubt that possibility and began pacing the floor. She was upset by the intrusion. No stranger ever came knocking on the door of Bourne Manor. Never. But if any ever did, they would venture cautiously and address Wysteria with a certain degree of apprehension and deference.

"Perhaps you should not spend so much time in your room and instead concern yourself with your work. There is plenty to keep you occupied, is there not?"

"Yes, Wysteria."

She eyed me curiously. "Hold out your hands," she demanded. I held them out to her. She examined them thoroughly, turning them over and checking for calluses. "Why will they not callus over?" she asked aloud. "They only blister and then crack. What a terrible nuisance." Still, after several minutes, she nodded, clearly appeased by my cracked and dried skin.

"There will be a new delivery of nets tomorrow," she said with satisfaction. "Sixty in all."

"Yes, Wysteria," I replied, but I did not feel the same oppression that normally accompanied such an exchange, for in my mind I could see clearly the boy's cap tipping in my direction, and I knew that regardless of Wysteria's dislike of intrusions, I would see him again.

6

I was awakened by a soft scratching, a creaking twist of branches. The limbs of the elm outside, bent down almost beyond their natural limit, were rubbing against my windowpane. Squirrels. They regularly rattled the branches and scurried along the ledges beneath the windows of the Manor. Spring was their season. Having nestled all winter in the holes and crevices that the house so amply provided, they had finally emerged and were busy training their young to search for food.

I wasn't bothered by their play. In fact, I often sat and watched them chase one another up and down the trunk of the great tree. I only feared for the birds, whose nests were frequently disturbed by the squirrels' exuberance. For, more than the squirrels, it was the birds that fascinated me.

Being so close to the lake, the grounds of Bourne Manor were home to an abundance of waterfowl—cormorants, ospreys, mergansers and herons—as well as raptors. Above the cliffs I had seen hawks and falcons, and once, a bald eagle, soaring over the harbor. But the birds closer to the Manor, the ones brave enough to nest within its walls, were the ones I viewed most intimately.

A pair of robins had, that particular spring, constructed a nest in the branches just beneath my window. I had watched as their babies hatched from their sea blue eggs and were carefully tended by the mother robin. I found myself at times wishing that I, too, had a mother who would tenderly look after me and patiently teach me to negotiate the breezes. But the boundedness of my life was far distant from the freedom of those winged creatures. I viewed them only from behind a thick layer of glass, for I spent a great deal of time merely looking out at life through the leaded panes of the Manor's multitude of locked windows.

Wysteria detested birds and squirrels and any other creatures that created a racket and disturbed her quiet. Her hearing was sharper than a knife and she was often irritated by the smallest of sounds.

"Miranda, what is that infernal ticking?"

I had to strain to hear what it was she referred to. "It's only the clock in the hall, Wysteria."

"Has it always been so offensive?"

"I've never noticed it before," I confessed.

"Close the door, Miranda," she commanded. "And let us return to some semblance of peace." I did as she requested.

"How is one to concentrate with all these disturbances?" I knew she referred not only to the clock in the hall, but also to the boy, for it was his disturbance that still lay heavy on her mind.

I, on the other hand, hoped for his return. I knew deep in my heart he would come. And to my delight, it was in fact the boy and not squirrels causing the disturbance in the elm.

Just above my window, the boy perched precariously on one of the upper limbs. I could not imagine how he had reached such a height, as there was a scarcity of branches the higher one climbed. I watched him as he attempted to reach the roof below the walk with his outstretched hand. Knowing the gap too wide to breach and unable to warn him through the closed window, I threw on a sweater, combed my fingers through my hair and ran quietly up the stairs to the glass house. I burst into the room, out onto the walk and peered over the railing.

"Oh, miss, it's you!" the boy said, startled by my sudden appearance. He looked up at me, a broad grin

spreading across his face. "I'm returning the kite as I said I would." I could now see the kite strapped securely to his back.

"That's honorable of you. And brave. But I'm afraid you'll never reach."

"Can you catch the tails, then, if I toss it to you?"

"It is too far a distance," I said. "Wait." I retrieved the anchor line and threw it down to him. "Tie the tail to the line, and keep your voice to a whisper." I nodded in the direction of the house to indicate Wysteria's presence within it.

"Quiet as a lamb, miss."

He undid the ties that held the kite to his back and then secured the tails to the line. I pulled it up and wrapped my fingers around the colorful ribbons, which the boy had artfully reattached. I held the railing with my free hand, realizing that in my haste I had forgotten to put on my boots and stood only in my stockinged feet. I placed the kite safely on the floor inside the glass house and closed the door.

"Safe home," the boy said with satisfaction.

I smiled.

"I'm Farley."

"Miranda," I said in turn.

"I'd shake your hand, if I could reach it."

"You'd lose your balance."

"I never do." He looked up, studying me curiously. I'm sure I must have appeared odd to him, with my wild hair and strange mix of clothes, for Wysteria had yet to sew me a proper spring coat, and I wore several layers of sweaters over the top of my night-dress. I smoothed out my hair and tried pulling it into a knot at the back of my head, but it was hope-less. The wind was too strong.

"I forgot my ribbon."

"It looks better that way," he said.

"It's too wild," I insisted.

"You live in this big house with only the old woman?" he inquired.

I nodded.

"Does she ever let you out?"

"Yes, of course," I said, though I realized this was not true. Wysteria rarely let me out any longer, not even to accompany her to town, but it seemed impor-tant that this boy not think me a captive.

"Can you come to the beach with me, then, to fly the kite? It's a much better run you'll get along the sand."

"I'd like that," I said, "but I'm not allowed out on my own."

"Why ever not?"

"It's rather difficult to explain."

Just at that moment, the bell rang. Never had Wysteria rung the bell at that hour of the morning.

"Is that the old woman? Does she know I'm here?"

"Perhaps."

"May I come back, miss?"

"Yes, I'd like that. But don't let Wysteria or the Hounds see you. Neither favor strangers."

He smiled. "I'm as quick as a hare in the brush and twice the man besides."

"I hope so." I started to leave and then turned back. The boy was still looking up at me. He took off his cap.

"Thank you," I said. "For bringing the kite back. It's a special kite, you know?"

"I know, miss, 'tis very special."

By the time I reached Wysteria, the bell was no longer ringing and I knew immediately she had no knowledge of Farley's presence. She was in her own room, bent over in a chair, recovering from a bad fit of coughing. She could not yet speak but held out her hand to me. The hand was bony, the skin over it like tissue paper, harboring rivers of veins that rose up blue and magenta against the pale surface.

As I waited for Wysteria to catch her breath, I stole a quick glance about the room. I was rarely allowed inside Wysteria's bedchamber. She never rang for me from there, only from the great room, and her door was always locked. It was smaller than I had imagined, and modestly furnished except for the bed, a giant four-poster with curtains draped around it, an ornate nightstand cluttered with myriad bottles and small jars and, against the far wall, an enormous armoire, which held her many black dresses. Though Wysteria apparently had little love for her deceased husband, she had carried her mourning well past the usual duration, the captain having been gone now more than twenty years. Still she continued each day to dress in her widow's weeds, which afforded her a certain status in town and provided her protection from any man interested in acquiring her assets.

"I prefer black," she always insisted. "It is neither boisterous nor plain and accompanies one anywhere with elegance."

"But do you not grow weary of wearing the same color?" I had asked once.

"Never. It is a mark of distinction." Wysteria's nightgown was the only piece of clothing she owned that was not black but instead a crisp white linen.

"Miranda," she whispered, clutching at the night-dress and pressing her hand firmly upon her chest. "I can barely find my breath." She looked up at me. Her eyes hollow and dark. I had never seen her in such a state, and it frightened me. As much as Wysteria bossed me about and kept me from the open air, she was the only semblance of family I had, and I could not possibly do without her. She collected and delivered the nets; she kept the Manor running. She was my only companion in that drafty house. As well, Wysteria, as long as I had known her, had always maintained a firm grasp on her own health, refusing to bow down to illness or surrender to infirmity. She wished never to appear weak in any regard or to cast a single doubt upon her ability to govern her affairs.

"Should I steam some water and bring a towel?" I asked.

"Yes," she whispered. "Do that."

For the rest of the morning and well into the late afternoon, I brought bowls of hot water and made a tent over Wysteria's head so she could take in the moist air. By the time her breathing finally eased, the sun was beginning to set and I left her to go light the lantern.

As I struck the match and lit the wick, I noticed on the beach below a small fire built close to the cliffs. Although I strained my eyes, I could make out no figure beside it. Perhaps it was Farley or one of the fishermen who slept outside, for I had heard that some did in good weather, liberating themselves from the shacks on the pier. Wysteria had warned me never to traverse the beach at night for this very reason, for the men were often drunk and out of their heads and could bring harm upon a young girl. I am not sure why she told me this, as she knew I never left the Manor alone even in the daytime.

Looking down upon the warm and glowing fire, I felt a glimmer of hope. Perhaps I was not entirely alone and the person making the fire was indeed a friend. I might signal to him and he would come and sit with me through the long night, helping Wysteria breathe until the sun rose.

Though I kept a light burning to guide others safely in off the water, I had never signaled distress from the Manor itself. Tentatively, I moved my hand in front of the lantern's flame, blocking the light from view and then bringing it back again. I did this several times, deliberately altering the rhythm and duration of light and darkness. I had no idea what I was doing, only hoping the tender of the fire might see my signal and possibly inquire as to its meaning. I waited for a response, but none came.

Gradually the fire on the beach died down and the wind came up, surrounding me in that little see-through house so far away from the world, so far from any kind of human warmth and comfort. As the growing darkness moved across the lake, I slowly closed the latch on the lantern and descended back into the Manor.

7

Farley did not return and Wysteria grew worse. There was no indication that anyone had seen my signal or if they had any idea how to interpret it. Every morning I ran to the walk, looking for Farley's red cap along the beach. I even checked the tops of all the trees about the Manor in hopes that I would spot him hanging out of one, but the days passed and still he did not come. Perhaps he'd heard the stories about the Manor and had had a change of heart. Perhaps he had learned something more about Wysteria or myself and now felt it too dangerous or foolish to set foot on the property.

I was accustomed to isolation and solitude, to spending hours with only my thoughts and the nets to occupy me. But since the day Farley had returned the kite, I had experienced a new and strange feeling I could only define as loneliness. I felt it everywhere I went. I grew listless and uneasy, and even found myself missing Wysteria's nagging and sour disposition, though it was not her company I craved.

One morning in early May, Wysteria's condition turned grave. She was unable to rise from her bed, even to lift her head from the pillow to drink. She was delirious with fever and called out bizarre commands to me. "Get my bannock!" she yelled. "Fill the lake water with tide!"

"Wysteria," I pleaded, trying to settle her, "you're not yourself. Please, lie back and rest and I will bring you a cool cloth."

It became clear to me as I placed the cloth on her burning forehead that I must do something, for it was evident that I could no longer continue to care for her on my own.

"I must find a doctor," I said, pouring a glass of water and urging her to drink.

She pushed it away from her parched lips. "No! No!" she protested. "No doctor. He won't come. The doctor was called, but the lady wasn't home. Fill the water. Fill the tide," she raved.

I placed the glass back on the nightstand and held her firmly by the shoulders, looking intently into her watery gray eyes. "Wysteria." She stared back, hot with fever. "Wysteria, look at me!"

"Who are you?"

"I'm Miranda."

"Where have you come from? What are you doing here?" Her raving frightened me.

"I live here, Wysteria. You found me. Remember?" She looked at me blankly.

"I must go to town for help. Do you understand?" She did not. "I will leave you for only a short while and return as quickly as I am able. Two of the Hounds will remain here with you and two will come with me." I did not wish to abandon her in such a state, but she needed a doctor, that was certain. She should have seen one days earlier. I had put off taking any action in hopes that she would recover. I feared now that she would suffer from my delay.

I made her drink from the glass of water and laid an extra blanket over her. "Hush now," I said, as if to a small, unruly child. "Do not fret, I will return with help." She settled back into sleep and I gathered two of the Hounds, positioning them close to her bedside and ordering them to stay. Then I took the other two and tied the thick leather leashes to their collars. I dressed in my heaviest wool coat, though the day was warm. The coat and my boots, along with the Hounds, would hopefully protect me from the wind.

$$\backsim$$

Much time had passed since I had walked unaccompanied in the world, and I feared I would lack the fortitude to face it. Those first few steps away from the Manor, I admit, were difficult ones. It was as if a strong magnet pulled at my heels. I was overcome with dread at leaving the protection of the Manor's walls and at the same time longed to be free of its grasp. Yet once I stepped beyond the shadow of the massive oak doors and through the front gates, my courage was renewed.

The day being mild and the Hounds knowing the way, I was able to walk freely and quite quickly down the long driveway to the railroad bed. The Hounds pulled endlessly on their leashes, but I held firm. They had caught a scent along the tracks that pleased them, and this kept them on course.

The air was full of the smell of hyacinth and elderberry flowers, the ground soft and muddy in places, and the fields, now free from the grip of snow and ice, prepared themselves once again for the growth of a new season.

As the Manor disappeared from sight and its grip

on me loosened, the open air and the aromas consumed my senses. This happened so suddenly and thoroughly that even the image of Wysteria in her desperate state fell away, replaced only with thoughts of spring. Had I not had the Hounds with me, I might have forgotten my mission altogether, so entranced was I with the beauty and freedom of the outdoors.

In the flat terrain near the lake, ospreys resided, building their giant nests at the very tops of the dead pines. I waited each year for the first glimpse of these regal birds. I loved to watch them patrol the shore, diving for fish with their great talons poised and ready for the catch. I found them loyal and steadfast, for they returned each year with the same partner to the same nest, adding to its breadth until the tops of the trees resembled giant broad-brimmed hats.

As there was yet no sign of the ospreys, I turned my attention fully to the journey at hand and proceeded down the rails at a steady pace. I kept my focus on our forward progression, guiding the Hounds around the numerous bends and keeping my eyes upon the tracks. We moved along smoothly until the Hounds stopped short and I looked up to see several figures walking toward us. Had I known a shorter way or a trail through the brush, I would have taken

it to avoid an encounter, but I could not risk being led off course and getting lost in a thicket with Wysteria in such dire need.

It was a group of six or seven boys, and I knew that in a very short time, they would spot us and block our way, as the railbed was narrow and the banks dropped off steeply from the sides. And indeed, that is how it happened.

"Who is that?" I heard one of the boys shout to the others upon catching sight of me.

"It's the Bourne Mouse," another answered. They walked closer to examine me, but not too close; I could tell they feared the Hounds. When they had reached a sufficient proximity, a stout and sullen-looking boy with a scarf loosely tied about his neck, obviously the leader of the small group, stepped forward.

"Does the Mouse speak?" he inquired. Why he addressed me by this strange name and spoke to me in such a disrespectful manner, I could not comprehend.

I looked up at him and the rest of the boys. They were, of course, taller than I, bigger in every way, and I could see now that my nickname was familiar to them, though my face was not. They were most likely the sons of local fishermen who lived on the pier. I surmised that, like me, they were outcasts in their own way. They had been teased and struck and hardened. I could see it in their eyes. They felt it their right to tease and strike in return anyone smaller than them, as if size were in itself a reason for punishment.

"Let us pass," I said, boldly lifting my chin and nodding to the Hounds, for they were the reason for my courage.

"Maybe we can help you, Little Mouse."

"I don't think so.

"Tell us where you're going in such a hurry."

I shook my head.

"Then you cannot pass."

The Hounds began to growl and the boys stepped back.

"I am going to find a doctor, if you must know."

"Are you ill?"

"No. Not for me."

"Is it the Witch? Is the Witch sick?"

"I don't understand what you mean," I said, though I supposed they referred to Wysteria.

"The Witch of the Manor. The old woman. The one who keeps you as her slave."

"I am no slave," I protested, and the boys laughed.

"That's right. You are her heir. Her Highness the Mouse." They all bowed deeply.

I narrowed my eyes at them.

"Don't tease her," one warned. "She might curse you like the Manor is cursed." With this comment, they drew back and regarded me more seriously.

"I don't believe in curses."

"You should," the stout boy said. "The Manor in which you live harbors a great and cursed fortune, and anyone who tries to claim it is driven mad. That house kills all that come to it. It keeps them bound until they suffocate inside its walls, or sends them hurtling over the cliffs, like the captain."

"I don't know what you're talking about."

"My father told me of it," the boy retorted.

"What did he tell?" But the boy would say no more.

"They are just stories," I said.

"Some stories are true."

"Some are not," I replied.

"Why are you so unnaturally small?" another boy interjected, regarding me as if I represented a strange and rare species.

"Because the Witch put a spell on her so she wouldn't grow," said one tall boy. "So the old widow can pick her up by the collar and toss her about. Place her on the mantel as a decoration." They all laughed.

"She's the little heir girl."

"So little you can barely see her." They laughed again, but with a certain wariness, for just at that moment the Hounds began to growl more fiercely and push forward.

"Let me pass," I said again. "If you do not, I will set my dogs upon you."

The Hounds were eager and the boys backed away.

"Let her pass," a smaller boy chirped, and the rest of the boys grumbled and stepped aside.

My legs shook as I walked by them, their jeers following me down the tracks until I turned off onto the main road. Once I was out of sight, I stopped to collect myself and bent down to the Hounds.

"Thank you," I whispered, and patted each on the head. "I would not have had the courage to face them without you." The Hounds wagged their tails and licked my face, then resumed pulling forward on their leashes.

The rest of the way to town, the boys' words jostled about in my mind. What had they meant about the captain? He had drowned in a storm on the lake. Everyone knew that. The Manor had not killed him. They were full of lies. It was rubbish. Wysteria was certainly strange, and the Manor forbidding in appearance, but people feared what they didn't know and went about making up fables and stories.

As for the fortune, I knew there was no truth to that. Wysteria had searched every crevice of the Manor to no avail. "Do you think, Miranda, that if there was a fortune inside these walls, I would bother for one moment with the mending of nets? Certainly not!"

"Stories," Wysteria had said. "Rumors. The working of idle minds." That was all there was to it. Nothing to fear. Nothing to go on about. How silly to think that the Manor, in which I had lived these many years, could harm anyone.

At the edge of town, I tied the Hounds to a thick tree trunk and left them a handful of biscuits to feast upon.

"I will return shortly," I assured them. "Do not howl or make a nuisance of yourselves while I am gone." I had heard Wysteria talk to them in much the same manner and they always obeyed. I hoped that in her absence they would do the same.

I had no idea where I might find the doctor, though I knew the town had one. I had seen his carriage driving by once when I'd accompanied Wysteria to the shops. She had nodded in his direction and identified him as the town's physician, though she had appeared nervous at the sight of him and had quickly turned her head away.

As much as possible, I kept to the back streets and

alleys, but I could not entirely avoid the curious stares of the shopkeepers and the jeers of a few schoolboys on their way home for lunch. The town was not large, but it was large enough that I had to ask several people for directions to the doctor's office.

Dr. Mead was his name, and he resided in a small house near the center of town. His office occupied the first floor, and although the door was open, he was not in. His nurse directed me to sit and wait, as he was expected back after lunch, but I could not. The Hounds would not remain patient for long, and every moment away from Wysteria meant she could lapse into a coughing spell and not recover. I let the nurse know the urgency of the matter.

"The doctor is out on the islands," she informed me briskly. "He is visiting a patient and there is nothing I can do to bring him back sooner than he intends to return." She was a tall woman with broad shoulders. Her face, which perhaps had once been pretty, was drawn and weary. Lines of worry marked her forehead. She nervously fussed about the office, visibly uncomfortable with my presence. She gazed at the ceiling or the ground when she spoke to me, but when she thought I wasn't looking, she openly stared, as if recording for some future use the exact details of my size and manner.

"Please," I said. "I must go back and see to Mrs. Barrows. Send the doctor as soon as he returns. It is urgent. I fear that without his help, she will not last the night."

"I will send him, but I cannot say that he will be pleased to come. Many years have passed since he ventured down the road to that unfortunate dwelling, and he carries no good memories from his time there. I can guarantee you that it is the last place on earth he would wish to visit." Though I wondered greatly at her words, I did not have the luxury of time to stop and inquire further into her meaning.

"If he comes after dark, tell him to mind his step, as the earth is soft in places about the Manor and his horse may find it difficult to navigate. I will light the lantern for him."

"Dr. Mead will come," she said, looking about anxiously. "You can be sure he will come."

8

"I wish you had found me sooner, young lady," Dr. Mead scolded. The doctor was a stately gentleman with a broad white mustache, prominent forehead, and thick heavy brows, which gave him the appearance of being either greatly surprised or greatly disappointed by some important matter. His whole demeanor was that of a man who had never spent a moment unconcerned with life or death. I even sensed that the subject of his dinner conversation would be of superior importance. This importance rose from him in waves, and I found myself walking a step or two behind him from the moment he entered the foyer of the Manor.

"She is in no condition to be moved, that is certain," he proclaimed upon removing the stethoscope from Wysteria's chest. "She has pneumonia. Do you know what that is?"

"Yes, sir. An affliction of the lungs."

"It is that indeed, and a bad case besides. Any move might well do her in. She must remain here until the fever breaks. But she cannot stay with only a young girl to care for her." The doctor took Wysteria's frail wrist in his hand, closed his eyes and counted her pulse. It was a strange sight to see a man in Wysteria's bedchamber, sitting on her bed and holding her hand without her consent.

Dr. Mead appeared to be an excellent physician, the kind of man who would sit by the bedside of a sick patient long into the night without complaint, but in Wysteria's presence, I could not help feeling that he was merely going through the motions of doctoring and wished desperately to be somewhere else.

I stared at the two of them, wondering if they had ever spoken to one another. They lived in the same town, so they must have met, but Wysteria called no one friend, and why should the doctor be any exception?

Dr. Mead removed his fingers from Wysteria's wrist and regarded me. "I do not have to tell you that your mistress's condition is grave. Is there a relative who can be summoned?" he asked.

"It is just Wysteria and I, sir, as I have no relations that I know of." The doctor's massive brows rose as he turned his full attention to me, inspecting me from head to foot.

"You are indeed as small as they say."

I nodded.

"Perhaps you will still grow."

"It is my hope, sir."

"Even if you were larger than average for your age and sturdy as an ox, I would not leave a girl to this work." The doctor rose and deposited his stethoscope in his bag. "I would send my nurse, but she will not come. No one will come out here." He paused, as if resigned to the words that followed. "Therefore, I will come myself each day until Mrs. Barrows is well enough to be taken to St. Elias's. Until that time and until I return, you must stay at her side. Hold a cold cloth to her head and rub her feet vigorously." He pulled back the blanket at the end of the bed, exposing Wysteria's stockinged feet. "Like this." He took one foot between his massive hands and rubbed it roughly. "We must draw the fever down from her head. Do you understand?"

I nodded.

"Let's see you try, then."

I walked to the edge of the bed and gingerly took Wysteria's thin foot from his hands.

"Don't be afraid of it, girl," he barked. I held it more firmly. It was bony like her hand, bony and cold. "Feel how cold it is?"

"Yes, sir. Like ice."

"You have your work cut out for you. Rub both feet until they are hot in your hands. Keep at it, and when you must stop to rest, make yourself useful by giving the poor woman something to drink. Make sure she drinks."

If Wysteria had been of sound mind, she would have dismissed the doctor for his impertinence, reminding him that she was no longer a poor woman and that he need not waste his pity upon her. But she was not up to rebuke and was so terribly frail that I was afraid to let the doctor leave me alone with her.

"Must you depart so soon, Dr. Mead?"

The doctor turned to me and his manner softened. "I do not envy you your place in this household," he said. "The heir, is that what they call you?"

"Yes, sir. But I am no heir."

"You are wise in not coveting the title, for no good has ever come from trying to claim this dwelling. Yet may I say that, if circumstances were otherwise, you would make a noble heir? You must be commended for your bravery, if nothing else."

"Thank you."

"Keep your courage, young lady. Do not let doubts

· 67 ·

creep in." He snapped his bag shut and looked warily about the room. "Though I know it is the nature of this house to breed doubt." He picked up his coat and hat and searched in vain for his gloves. "Are there no lights in this dreary abode?"

I took a match and lit the candle on the nightstand and one in the window.

"Good. And perhaps you can throw another log on the fire. The dankness alone in this place would drain the life out of a soul."

"Yes, sir." Dr. Mead had arrived before sunset, and as the house had grown darker, he had become increasingly anxious.

"I'll be off, then." I lit another candle and handed it to him as we walked to the foyer.

"Those beasts—will they let me pass?" he said, putting on his hat.

"Yes, sir. I will keep them inside so they will not frighten your horse."

"I am grateful."

"Safe journey home, sir," I said as I opened the door for him, letting in a strong draft of damp spring air.

"Yes. And a good night to you, young lady."

I watched the light from Dr. Mead's candle wind its way down the long drive and then go out as he mounted his horse and rode away.

The doctor came as promised each morning to check on Wysteria's progress and to administer medicine from his store of small glass bottles. Though he was stern, he was also generous with his time, and I appreciated his presence in the house. I had not, in memory, known any men, for no father or uncle of my own could I recall. All men must be like this, I thought as I watched the doctor enter the Manor and move confidently around the sitting room, whisking off his great, dark cape and hanging it over the banister. He gave off a faint but deeply masculine scent of the woods and pipe tobacco.

With each visit, the doctor seemed more at ease within the Manor, and after a while he would even accept a cup of tea and linger in the sitting room, looking about at the furnishings and discussing his knowledge of art and the finer things of life.

Though he was generally guarded in his speech and would not dwell on any one topic, on occasion he would inquire about my life, and I could often lead him to subjects I wished to know more about.

"And what of your schooling?" the doctor asked one day as I poured his tea.

"I take my schooling at home, sir."

"I see. I did the same, and just as well. It harmed me none. Is it Mrs. Barrows who is your teacher?" I nodded. "And what do you spend your time learning?"

"Sums . . . geography, history."

"Do you know the history of this house, then?"

"Only what folks say."

"And what do folks say?"

"That the house is cursed, sir."

The doctor paused and looked at me, his right eyebrow rising into a high arch.

"Is it true, sir?"

"Some believe it."

"And you, sir?"

" 'Curse' is a convenient term used for things one does not understand. Perhaps those who inhabit a dwelling curse it themselves by the way they act. There have been many unhappy unions in this house over the years. Many a marriage turned sour because of a belief in curses."

"The captain and Wysteria?"

"Yes. And others before them."

"Did you know Captain Barrows?" Dr. Mead hesitated, and I thought he might suddenly end the conversation as he had done on previous visits when the subject made him uncomfortable, but he continued to speak.

"Our families were never on good terms, but Barrows and I met at school. We had the kind of friendship forged in boyhood, based upon one's ability to catch frogs and successfully skip stones across the bay. He was a kind boy and an honest man, a man who could do many things well and a few things excellently, but an impractical dreamer above all else. Like his father, and his father before him."

"Is it not a good thing to be a dreamer, sir?"

"Not when one believes in things that can never be," he replied sternly.

"What do you mean?"

Dr. Mead sighed and walked over to the window.

"Material wealth meant nothing to him," the doctor said, clearly frustrated by this quality in his friend. "He cared only about the sea and later about his bride, which was perhaps the most tragic of all."

"Why is that, sir?"

"Captain Barrows believed that if he married for love—and he did love his wife, though I could never understand why—he would break the curse that hung over this wretched house. He never gave up hope that his wife would one day return his affections. All of his voyages drew him back here in an attempt to win her heart. In the end, he wished to liberate them both from the grasp of Bourne Manor, to sell this place once and for all, but he was foiled even in that. He could not accept that his wife's allegiance was never to him. I tried to counsel him against the marriage from the beginning, but he would not listen."

"Why would you be against it, sir?"

"Your mistress was courted by every eligible bachelor in town, including myself, but none pleased her. This is what she wanted," he said, sweeping his hand about the room. "Bourne Manor was always foremost in her thoughts. She never took her eyes from it. Mrs. Barrows is not a woman who is capable of love. Surely you have found this yourself."

I nodded.

"Perhaps it is the remoteness of this place that preyed upon her as it preyed on those before her. Isolation may be the only curse that exists here. Though I do not believe her incapacity for human affection was a product of solitude. I suspect that it began early on."

"Sir?"

"I'm not sure how much you know of your mistress's past, but Mrs. Barrows was dreadfully poor once. So poor, her family could not afford even the bare essentials. Poverty is no crime, mind you. Many a noble man has come into this world with nothing and made an honorable place for himself. But in Mrs. Barrows's case, the effects were . . ." The doctor's voice trailed off.

"What, sir?"

"All I shall say is that your mistress always knew she would live here one day. It was perhaps the one thing she knew in all her life. It mattered little how she came to own Bourne Manor or how she kept it." He held my gaze. "Poverty can steal away more than physical comfort. It can lead one to act without integrity; let no one tell you otherwise." The doctor glanced briefly out at the lake.

The weather was turning. Clouds were gathering over the islands. "It is, in my opinion, young lady," he said, "better not to dream."

"Shall we see to Mrs. Barrows, then?"

"Yes, Dr. Mead."

Together we walked up the stairs to Wysteria's room. Dr. Mead adjusted her covers and laid the inside of his wrist on her forehead, checking for fever. He touched her lightly, as one might touch a china doll one had long ago lost interest in and now pitied.

"Sir?" I knew I must ask one more question while he was in the mood for conversation.

"Yes?"

"Did the captain die, sir, as the stories say? On this lake, in a storm?" In the previous days, I had found myself thinking of the story the boys on the tracks had told me and wondering if it was true.

There suddenly seemed to be so many things I did not know the truth about.

"You are curious about him?"

"Yes, sir."

"What do you know of him?"

"Only that he was a sea captain and traveled the world. He made maps and built boats. He spoke several languages."

"You seem to know more than most. Has Mrs. Barrows told you all these things?"

"Oh, no, sir. She never speaks of him."

"I see."

I lowered my voice to a whisper, though I could hear Wysteria's steady breathing. "I have spent time in the captain's study, sir. But please do not mention it to Wysteria. She would not approve."

"You need not worry, child. Your secret is safe with me."

"Thank you, sir."

"Do you spend much time in this study of his?"

"Yes, sir. It is the brightest of all the rooms. Indeed, it is my favorite room in all the Manor."

"And what is it you do there?"

"I sit mostly, sir, and read. I look at the captain's books. He has many fine books about seabirds and shipbuilding."

"And these subjects interest you?"

"Yes, sir. I also spend my time watching the weather and . . ."

I stopped myself, for I did not think it proper to mention the kites to him.

"Yes?"

"Observing the birds and wildlife on the beach."

"It sounds like a fascinating place from which to observe life."

"It is, sir."

"I would very much like to see this study, if you think it appropriate."

"Of course, sir. You were his friend. You knew him better than I."

"Would you be so kind as to show it to me?"

"Now, sir?"

"Yes, if it is convenient."

I could see no reason why the doctor should not accompany me. All the kites were in the glass house or the attic, and they were the only things I wished to keep from him.

"I would be happy to show it to you, sir."

Wysteria moaned and turned over in her sleep. Dr. Mead adjusted her covers again and put a cool cloth on her head, then eagerly followed me to the third floor. He watched intently as I took the skeleton key from my pocket and fitted it into the lock.

"It seems you have discovered more than just the captain's study. You must know all the secrets of this place by now, an intelligent girl like yourself?"

"Oh, no, sir. I know very little, as Wysteria holds the keys to the rest of the Manor."

I pushed open the door and held it for the doctor, then walked over to the windows and drew back the curtains for more light, but the sky was now completely overcast. Rain threatened, and the room remained in shadow. I lit a lantern on the desk instead so that the doctor could have a proper view of things.

"Ahhh." Dr. Mead sighed, stepping across the threshold. "In all the years I knew the captain, I never set foot inside. It was his private study, you understand. I'm not sure what he would think of our being here, or of a young lady like you knowing his deepest secrets."

"What secrets do you mean, sir?" I felt my face grow hot.

"The secrets that a house such as this harbors. The captain spoke to me of one such secret, though I did not believe him at the time. There are, as you know, many stories that dance around in people's minds about this place, regarding hidden fortunes and such." He ran his fingers across the top of the captain's desk, fingering lightly the papers and maps upon it. He walked to the fireplace and picked up a small glass globe with a sailing ship inside. He moved it about in his hands. His mood grew pensive and somber as he examined the globe, and a peculiar light appeared in his eyes when again he spoke.

"It is strange how life is so like a circle, is it not? How a thing can come around once again?"

"Sir?"

"Perhaps not all is lost. Perhaps it might still be redeemed." The doctor replaced the globe on the mantel. "May I?" he asked, walking over to the captain's spyglass and tipping it up to his eye.

"Yes, sir. You can see the islands quite well in fair weather."

"It is an excellent spot. A clear view. I can see why you like it here. It is quite different from the rest of the house."

"Look, sir," I said, turning the spyglass ever so slightly to the north, "you can see the light at Bolton Island from here, even in the gloom."

"Ah, yes. Quite nice." The doctor seemed entranced by the view, and when the Hounds began to bark from the floor below, he flinched, his reverie suddenly broken. "Those beasts!"

"Perhaps Wysteria has awoken?"

"Yes," he said, checking his watch. "I will see to Mrs. Barrows, then make my way back to town. I have quite overstayed my time."

Wysteria was, as before, deep in sleep. The Hounds had only been barking at the wind, which they often did. They were now stretched out peacefully on the floor beside her bed, and glanced up as we walked into the room. One stretched his neck and licked the laces of my boots. Dr. Mead noticed.

"And are these the famous boots that keep you anchored here?" the doctor inquired.

"Yes, sir."

"I wish you a brighter fate than Captain Barrows's." I must have appeared shocked at his words, for he suddenly changed his tone.

"I'm afraid that I have fallen prey to the melancholy of these walls. Perhaps I should not speak so to a young lady, though I sense you are stronger than your physical dimensions indicate. I only wish I had spoken as adamantly to my friend while there was time to do so." The doctor opened the curtains around Wysteria's bed and stood looking down at her.

"The fever is waning. You've done well. I believe

Mrs. Barrows is strong enough to transport to the hospital."

"She will not like it, sir."

"She has no choice. I will come with my stewards and collect her this very afternoon."

"If you think it best, Dr. Mead."

"I do," he said, gathering up his bag. "And what of you, little one? What will you do? It may be longer than a fortnight before her return."

"I must stay to light the lantern and watch over the Hounds, sir. I cannot abandon them. There are many nets, too, that I have yet to mend. I cannot imagine how we will pay you for your services if I do not remain here."

"There is no hurry. If nothing else, Mrs. Barrows has a reputation for paying her debts."

"Thank you, sir."

"You assure me that you will be fine, then? Shall I take you at your word?".

"Yes. I am used to being alone."

He frowned and put his hand on my shoulder. "For a brief time, I will allow it, but I'll come when I can to check on you. In the meanwhile, light the lantern each night as usual. That will be a sign to me that all is well."

"Yes, of course. Thank you, sir."

"Thank you, young lady, for showing me the captain's study. It meant more to me than you can know. I suspect there is much there still to see. I would like to visit it again, if I may."

"Certainly," I said, and walked him to the door.

"You are a curious little thing," he remarked before departing. "Curious indeed."

9

The days following Wysteria's departure were lonely, the nights long and fretful. Outside, a strange fog settled over the cliffs, lingering in the gullies and spreading out over the fields. Dr. Mead could not make his way out to me each day as he had promised, for the air had become dense and impenetrable. I did not venture past the front gates of the Manor myself, as I could not see beyond my own hand. I pitied any sailor caught out on the lake in such weather. A mist that thick could close in and envelop a boat in its impervious vapor for hours, parting only long enough to display a small circumference of water and no land in sight.

Perhaps it was the mist that obscured my thoughts, for like a sailor caught in its spell, I could think only that I was bound to the Manor forever and could not see my way free of it.

As well, I had discovered in Wysteria's absence that the Manor was plagued by strange noises after dark, and the Hounds bayed and howled at the walls as if something lingered inside them, wishing to escape. I consoled myself with the knowledge that fog often produces odd echoes, catching and holding sounds and throwing them far off to betray the senses, and that the Hounds were known on occasion to bark at their own shadows. Still, I could not dismiss my mounting sense of unease at the thought that the Manor was mourning the loss of its mistress and in its grief had turned its full attention upon me, wrapping me firmly in its gloom.

On nights when I fell into a deep enough sleep, my dreams were disturbed by shadows of dark creatures and oppressive forces, and I often woke feeling as if the walls themselves were alive and pressing in upon me. At such moments, I would stand up and walk about my room to convince myself it was not true. By the time morning arrived, I would have vowed to leave the Manor and never return, to take my chances in the fog, but by afternoon I could not imagine why I had felt so, and chastised myself for ever having entertained a desire to flee.

It was during this time that I once again saw the

fire on the beach. This was most uncommon—not only that someone would choose to make camp there during such foul weather, but that I could see the fire at all through the bleakness. In the drifting mist I caught distinct glimpses of it. The same fire, the same spot. When I opened the front door to let the Hounds out, I caught the scent of woodsmoke as it drifted inland on the faint and lifeless breeze.

I kept the lantern burning through the day, as was done in the case of fog, but I did not attempt to signal again to the maker of the fire, for I did not know to whom I signaled, friend or foe. Although the fire offered me hope that I was not entirely alone, a strange feeling had begun to sweep over me that perhaps there was no one besides myself that I could trust or turn to.

One afternoon, while calling the Hounds in for supper, I noticed, in the parting of the fog, a figure standing out beyond the gates, at the very end of the drive. I waited for it to move, thinking at first that it must be Dr. Mead come to visit, but the specter stood as still as a statue, gazing up at the widow's walk. I strained my eyes to bring its form into focus. It appeared to be a woman—or the ghost of a woman, for what woman would come out to the Manor in such weather?

Perhaps in my isolation I had lost my sense of reason, but I felt that I must know whether this apparition was real or not. I leashed one of the Hounds and made my way to the front gate.

"Can I help you?" I yelled into the mist.

The figure turned in my direction and walked slowly toward me. As it neared, I saw to my great relief that it was made of flesh and bone and that it was in fact Dr. Mead's nurse, whom I had met at his office. She stood stoically before me, wrapping a scarf tightly about her neck against the dampness.

"Miss Moreland," she said, nodding as a means of introduction.

"Yes. I remember."

"I have come in the doctor's stead to inquire after your welfare." She held out a small basket from her side and presented it to me. "Dr. Mead sends you turnips and apples. Enough for a simple soup."

"Thank you," I said, taking the basket. "Tell him that I am fine, and grateful for his kindness."

Miss Moreland made no response, her eyes staring beyond me to the Manor.

"Is the doctor well? I haven't seen him in some time."

"Yes, he is well," she answered nervously. "He is very busy, with little time for errands . . . in places such as this."

"I see." The details of my first meeting with Dr.

Mead's nurse came to mind, and I was suddenly wary of her. Her expression in the dimness was even more strained than I remembered, her skin sallow and weathered, yet there was a sincerity in her manner I could not deny.

"Do you wish to come in, Miss Moreland? I could make tea."

"No." She appeared to bristle at the very suggestion. "I will not step across the threshold of that dwelling. I will come no farther than the gate."

"Why is that?" I asked, steadying my voice, for something in her tone sent a chill through me. The Hound was growing restless at my side, but I was glad of his presence and did not release him.

"Surely you have not lived here these many years and not felt its pull upon you?"

"It is only a house, Miss Moreland. You speak as if it were a living thing."

"Some believe it to be so." At that moment, a veil seemed to drop before her eyes, and again she stared past me to the Manor as she spoke. "This house. Your mistress. They have destroyed others. They could destroy you."

"What do you mean?"

"They sent him to his death."

"Captain Barrows?"

"No storm took him. Of that you can be sure."

"The captain did not die on the lake?"

"He did not."

"How, then, Miss Moreland?" I was eager for her reply. Perhaps she would tell me what the doctor could not.

"Some thought he went mad over her," she said, "wandering the beach late at night, building fires and sleeping out in all weather. They say he threw himself off the cliffs in despair. He would not have been the first in his family to do so."

"I did not know."

"There is much you do not know, miss."

"Can you tell me more?"

She nodded. "When the captain's body was found washed up on the rocks, the coast guard declared his death a drowning, another casualty of the storm. Dr. Mead did not disagree."

"But you believe he should have?"

"If he had looked further, if he had not already made up his mind that the captain had merely followed in his family's footsteps, he would have found other reasons for the captain's death."

"And what would they be, Miss Moreland?"

"I cannot say. Only that she had a hand in it."

"But surely Dr. Mead would have—"

"Dr. Mead is a good man, but this house exacts a price from all who've had dealings with it, miss. The doctor is no exception. The Mead family is as deeply entangled in its history as the Barrowses."

"In what way?"

"The Meads were the original owners of this Manor. It was named after the doctor's great-grandmother Sylvia Bourne. Early on they lost it to the Barrows family over some misunderstanding. In the end, they lost not only the house, but supposedly the fabled fortune as well. It happened long ago, but I'm afraid the matter is still not laid to rest. He still cannot let it go."

"I do not understand. There is no longer any fortune. Surely Dr. Mead must realize that?"

"I do not know what he realizes, or what he covets. I know only that he will have no peace now until he finds whatever it is he seeks. Though he has stayed away these many years, the Manor has once again cast a shadow over him, and under its influence he cannot be trusted to think clearly." She steadied herself against the wind. "Please, miss. Promise me that you will not let him pass through the doors of Bourne Manor again," she pleaded.

"But this is my home you speak of, Miss Moreland."

"It is a dangerous place, miss. Leave it as soon as you are able. Do not wait for her return. If she could destroy her own husband, would she not do the same to you?"

"But—"

"I must go," Miss Moreland said, looking nervously about her. "I trust you will not tell the doctor of our conversation."

"No. Of course not."

"I bid you good day, then, miss," she said without meeting my eyes. And with that she was gone.

In the days that followed, I tried to make sense of Miss Moreland's words. Though they did not come together in any coherent way, I found I could not dismiss them as simply another story. Neither could I ignore one disturbing phenomenon: while I slept, the door of my room locked and then, shortly before dawn, unlocked on its own. This happened each night, though I never saw the key turn in either direction. I only discovered it when I woke in the early hours, attempting to make my way to the washroom at the end of the hall. I also distinctly heard something that resembled footsteps on the lower landing and once saw a light cast briefly under my door. I had always assumed that it was Wysteria who was responsible for the locking of the doors, but perhaps I had been wrong. I began to suspect that the rumors were true and that something indeed lingered in the house, though if it was a human spirit, I never saw or heard it in the daylight. I found that each time I thought of abandoning the Manor, the noises would grow louder. The more afraid I became, the more convinced I was that I must remain inside its walls.

One night while I lay in bed staring at the ceiling, Miss Moreland's strange tale filled my thoughts and led me to remember something Wysteria had once said about the Manor's being closed up properly at night. "It is imperative, Miranda, that every room be locked before bed and the ring of keys securely fastened to my side upon retiring." As the skeleton key could lock and unlock only the third-floor rooms, I was at a loss as to how to secure all the other doors. Since Wysteria had left the Manor, I had searched in vain for her keys. I knew there was a certain place she kept them after she retired at night, for as vigilant as she was, she would not have slept with them, and I also knew she had not taken them with her, as she had only worn a light coat over her dressing gown and Dr. Mead would have noticed.

There was one place that I had not looked, and

that was Wysteria's bedchamber. Even though I had spent much time there during her illness, I felt uneasy about entering it without her permission. Still, I had to find some peace, and so I made my way there as soon as it was light.

Nothing had changed since her departure. Bedsheets still lay rumpled and twisted, evidence of Wysteria's tossing about in her feverish state. I inspected her nightstand and looked under the bed. Lastly, I opened her armoire and pulled aside the many black dresses. On the floor was a wooden box, the top of which was engraved with the initials W.B. It was unlocked and I opened it. Inside lay Wysteria's keys. Relieved, I put them directly into my pocket and was about to close the box when I spied something at the bottom of it. Underneath a white handkerchief lay a series of small glass bottles turned on their sides. They were not unlike the ones that lined Wysteria's nightstand, only these looked much older and were empty but for one, which distinctly had my name written upon it in Wysteria's hand. I picked it up and examined it in the light. Below my name, there was a word scrawled upon the slender white label that I could not decipher but that looked very much like the writing on the few small bottles Dr. Mead had prescribed for Wysteria during her recent illness. I unscrewed the cap and sniffed, detecting only a slight fragrance of alcohol. Strange, I thought. Whatever could it be for? I replaced the cap and dropped the bottle in my pocket with the keys. I then examined each of the other bottles, but, as I had suspected, the labels all bore the same illegible scrawl. I explored the rest of the armoire. It was vast and deep, yet it held nothing but petticoats and old bed curtains, and so I closed it. I left Wysteria's chamber, locking the door behind me.

With keys in hand, I promptly locked every door and every cupboard as Wysteria did upon retiring for bed, and that night there were no noises or footsteps or lights. I locked myself into the captain's study in the evening after I lit the lantern, staying there until dawn, and the door remained secure until I myself opened it.

In my isolation, I had much time to ponder the nurse's story, the things Dr. Mead had told me about the captain and Wysteria, and the small glass bottle with my name on it, but no matter how I tried, nothing fit together properly. Perhaps they had nothing to do with one another. Perhaps they were just too many people's stories tangled about each other. How could I believe that Wysteria and the Manor would harm me? Wysteria had found me and taken me in. The

Manor had sheltered me. Yet Miss Moreland's words resounded in my ears: "Leave it as soon as you are able. . . . Do not wait for her return." I had the distinct feeling that I would never unravel this mystery while confined within the walls of the Manor, and so I promised myself that I would wait until the first clear day. Surely in the open air it would all make sense to me.

Just as I was to abandon all hope of ever leaving, the fog lifted, broken by a strong gale that raged against the glass and brought heavy rain that traveled in long, unbroken sheets across the lake. For two days, I could open the door only long enough to collect firewood from the box in the entranceway, but I preferred the rain to the fog, for now I had once again a view of the mountains.

By early June, I was sleeping through the night again, all the doors securely locked and the house quiet. I had found it difficult in the days previous to keep my concentration with the nets and had accomplished little. As well, I had grown short-tempered with the Hounds, and they had left my peevish company to take their chances in the fog. The day the weather finally cleared, the shaggy beasts came back humble and hungry, and with them they brought Farley.

10

"Up here! I'm up here!" Farley stood at the top of the elm above my window with a ribbon in his hand. "I came back, like I said I would. Here!" He held out the ribbon to me. "For your hair." I could barely hear him through the thick glass. I signaled that I would come up to the walk.

"You're back," I said, looking over the railing.

"Yes, miss. I'm back." A wide smile spread across his face. He held up the ribbon again. "A gift."

"Thank you," I said, lowering the anchor line. The ribbon was made of silk the color of summer wheat, and I immediately tied it into my hair. I was over-joyed to see Farley. I could not deny that his dis-appearance had caused me more sorrow than I had imagined possible.

"Where have you been?"

"Burlington. We brought up a new boat. That one out there," he said, pointing to a large schooner at the edge of the bay.

"You're not working today?"

He seemed surprised. "No, miss. I've been given the week off, but I wouldn't work today anyway. 'Tis Sunday."

"Oh, yes, of course." The days had flowed into one another, though even with Wysteria here, Sundays were as any other day might be. We mended nets when there were nets to mend. There was no going to church or reading the Bible for us; these practices were for common people, Wysteria said. We had no need of them.

"Don't you go to church, then?"

"No."

"Are you a heathen?"

"I don't think so. I know I'm not Catholic. Wysteria greatly dislikes Catholics."

Farley laughed. "Then she'd dislike me."

"Are you Catholic?"

"Me family is. I have me own ways, but I do go to church and keep at me prayers. Fishermen need more prayers than landlubbers like yourself. Praying can be a good thing." He gazed up at the Manor.

I nodded. "You've heard about this place?"

"I've heard the stories, but I don't go in for stories. Mostly I take things as they come to me, not secondhand."

"I see."

"Can you leave, then? Can you come to the beach and bring your kite?"

"I'm not sure." It surprised me to think that I would not jump at the chance to leave, but I felt that strange pull come over me, that dread at walking outside, as if my leaving were a betrayal. Perhaps, I thought, it wasn't Wysteria who kept me here, but the Manor that claimed my allegiance.

"Is it the old woman? Is that why you hesitate? Is she at home?"

"Wysteria? No. She's ill. She has been taken to the hospital."

"You're alone, then?"

"Dr. Mead stops by to check on me."

" 'Tis an awful big house to be alone in. I'd ask you to stay on the boat, but we're seven men and it's not a place for a lady, to be sure."

"Thank you, but I have to stay to watch the Hounds and light the lantern. It's our duty . . . for the boats on the lake."

"Can you not come out if I'm with you? I'll make sure nothing happens to you."

"Perhaps I can go for a short while, but I must be back before dark."

"That's grand." Farley clapped his hands and began climbing down the elm.

"I'll meet you outside the front door." I did not want Farley to come inside the Manor, to ever walk across its threshold. In some strange way, I knew it would not like Farley. Whatever brought me happiness, I was certain the Manor would disapprove of.

"Bring the kite," he yelled after me.

"I'll bring two if you like."

"You've more than one?"

"A whole roomful."

"Remarkable!" Farley scrambled down the tree. I ran to the walk and retrieved the Red Dragon and a large blue kite with feathers etched into its sides that I thought Farley would like. I dressed in my heavy coat and boots but left the Hounds inside so they wouldn't follow us and chase after the kites.

Farley and I spent the whole of that day together, the first of many to come. I had never played with any other children that I could remember and was unsure how one went about doing so, but Farley had an unending supply of ideas and plans, which occupied us into the late afternoon.

He was fascinated with kites and wings and everything to do with flight. He'd flown many kites with his brothers along the Irish coast, as that was where he had come from.

"A great green island," he said of it. "With mountains and streams, dragons and wee folk."

"Dragons?"

He laughed. "No. There are no more dragons, though people say they once roamed the high ridges. But there are wee folk still. Me cousin Leo saw one himself in the grove at St. Bernard's. They live in the valleys mostly, but they'll come out into the fields now and again."

"What are they?"

"Small folk. A quarter the size of yourself. Mischief makers, the lot of them, unless you find one with his stash of gold, catch him and tie him fast. Then you'll come out a rich man in the end, with no landlord to hover over you."

"It sounds like a fairy-tale place."

"It is . . . in a way. But it's a hard place, too."

"Are there all sorts of seabirds there?" I asked.

"By the ocean, you mean?"

I nodded.

"Get on with you. Have you never seen the ocean yourself?"

"Never."

"A girl like you? 'Tis criminal."

"Why do you say that?"

He adjusted the tension on the line and swung his leg over the rock on which he sat. "You can't imagine how many there are . . . like yourself. You can't imagine until you've seen it with your own eyes."

"What do you mean?"

"They're everywhere. Dodging and flying about. Small ones with tiny pencil legs and great big ones with beaks to beat the band."

"I don't understand."

"Don't you know what you are, girl?" I shook my head.

"You're a bird, for sure."

I laughed. "I am not."

"The ones deny it are the ones that are. Me gran in Donegal used to know one."

"I don't believe you."

"That's why you can't go out on your own, why you wear those boots, isn't it? So the wind won't take you?" I felt my face flush.

"They're all slight, like you, and bound to the

wind and in need of protection till they can find their way. Me gran said the one she knew got blown away while she was still too young to know." I couldn't believe what he was saying.

"I've known it from the start. You can't believe it yourself yet, only 'cause you haven't known."

"But I've never seen anyone else like me. I've never even heard of anyone who gets picked up by the wind."

"You haven't known who you are, so why would you look for others like yourself?"

"If what you say is true, where would I look?"

"Have you ever had a thought to go somewhere? Someplace you've never been?"

"I'm not sure."

"Aw, come on now. Don't you know?"

"Well, I've always wanted to go across the lake," I said, pointing to the opposite shore. "Close to the mountains. I had a dream once that I was sitting on that tall one. The one with the little bald spot gracing the top."

"Maybe the mountains are calling you. Maybe there are others there like you." His eyes lit up. "Maybe it's the place the wind is always trying to take you, only you're afraid to let it."

"How would I get there?"

"Fly."

"It's not like that, Farley. I don't fly. I just get picked up and the wind decides."

"Then you need wings."

I laughed again. "And where would I find wings?"

Farley pointed up to the sky at the Red Dragon and the Blue Devil, as he had named it. "There, miss," he said. "There are your wings."

11

I dreamt of wings. All through the night. Wings of birds and dragons and even the tiny wings of fire-flies. All beating at a constant rhythm. All open to the wind. I woke with the feeling of them about me, fluttering above my head, pulling at my shoulders, as if I too possessed appendages for flight.

I did not notice the day outside or even stop for breakfast but gathered as quickly as I could all the kites from the walk and those still remaining in the attic. Farley had proposed the idea that the kites might, if arranged properly, make a pair of wings. I could not imagine it but agreed to bring as many as I could. They were light but awkward, and I had to be careful not to trip on their strings and tear their delicate coverings as I descended the stairs to the main floor.

I let the Hounds out with me, holding on to their leashes for security, and hurried down to the lake.

It was a beautiful day, the sky clear and the breeze strong and warm. Farley was there, involved in some pressing concern in the sand.

"Come look at what I've made," he shouted. I let the Hounds loose and laid the kites on the sand, placing a heavy rock on them so they wouldn't fly away. Farley stood and stepped aside. He had crafted a house out of sand, an exact replica of the Manor, which towered above us.

"It's magnificent," I said.

"Why, thank you, miss." He took a bow.

"However did you make it?"

"You wet the sand and pack it down. It's best if you have a tin, like this," he said, pulling an empty square tobacco tin from his pocket. "And a bucket." He proudly displayed a rusty bucket he said he had found tangled in the driftwood.

"We'll make another one. One that's not so sad. This house . . . that house," he said, pointing up at the Manor, "it's sad."

"Yes," I said. "It is sad." It's more than sad, I wanted to say. It was full of something I didn't understand, something that drew me and at times made me want to run from it and never return.

"Farley?"

"Yes, miss."

"If you owned a dwelling such as the Manor, what would you do with it?"

"What do you mean, miss?"

"Would you live in it?"

"No, miss. I don't think it likes me."

"Would you sell it, then?"

"I think that would be the only thing to do."

"Yes," I said. "I think the captain, Wysteria's husband, wanted to sell it, too. At least, that is what the doctor said."

"But what of your mistress?"

"She would never have left it." Suddenly, I understood the captain's desire to be free of everything that had to do with the Manor, the curses and the rumors of madness and the ill-gotten fortune. And I also understood that Wysteria never would have allowed it. She would have stopped him any way she could.

"We'll wreck it."

"Oh, no. You've worked so hard."

"It's fun to wreck them. Then you can start over. Watch." Farley took the bucket from beside him, walked down to the water's edge and filled it to the brim. He poured the first bucket and I poured the second. After three bucketsful, the Manor had melted back into the beach, and I felt a surprising relief and joy at its demise.

"Now," he said. "Let's build a different sort of house."

"What sort?"

"Your dream house."

"I don't have a dream house."

"Every girl has a house of her dreams."

"A cottage," I said, remembering a tiny stone cottage I'd seen a long time ago in a storybook.

"Yes," he agreed. "Perfect. A neat white cottage with a cozy fire."

"And flowers in boxes beneath the windows."

"Just big enough for wee folk."

"Just big enough for me."

"Indeed."

We built a perfect little cottage out of sand with the help of Farley's tin and the rusting bucket, and some lichen we peeled from rocks for window-box flowers. We left it there all day, and when the tide came up, the waves refused to disturb it, only lapping away at the foundation enough to cement it more firmly to the beach.

The morning we spent with the kites, arranging them in different combinations and attempting to lace them to each other, but they were unwieldy, and as the wind was strong, we spent most of our time trying to keep them from flying off. By late morning, Farley had managed to arrange several of the paper kites into something that resembled a wing, for these were the ones sturdy enough to bear weight and had the appropriate clasps attached to them.

"The paper," Farley commented, "is like something I've seen before. It is strong in weave yet made so fine. Tough enough to endure the ravages of the wind, but light enough to ride upon it." I explained that the captain must have made his own paper with the screens in the attic, for the kites and all his maps were of the same grade and texture.

When we stopped for lunch, Farley suggested we store the kites inside a small enclosure that backed up to the cliffs. To call it a cave would have been extravagant, but there was enough of an opening that we could wedge the kites and the wing inside, where the wind could not find them.

Farley had brought a large loaf of bread, which was his ration for the week, and a few sardines wrapped in a plain cloth. I'd brought a canister of dried currants from the pantry. Wysteria saved currants for special occasions, which never came, as she did not celebrate any, not even Christmas. She doled them out in minute amounts to be sanctimoniously consumed on the first of May, when the captains made their spring payments, and late in the summer, once all the fleet owners had signed her on again for the coming year. When she returned to the Manor, she would undoubtedly search for them, and I would have to find a reason for their absence, for I planned that Farley and I would feast on them until the jar was empty and take whatever punishment was due me at a later date.

"Are you sure you can spare these?" Farley asked.

"Yes. It's a special occasion. That's what they're for." He smiled and poured out a handful. In a playful and distinctly boyish manner, he lay back, popping the currants into the air and catching them in his mouth.

"What will you do when you grow up?" I inquired.

Farley laughed. "Why, miss, I'm already grown up enough to work. But I don't want to be at sea forever, that's for certain."

"I thought you liked sailing?"

"I like the boats, miss. I like the clean, fresh smell of the open water. But I don't like to pull up more fish than I need, or to obey the orders of another man."

"What will you do, then?"

"Maybe I'll build kites and sell them to people all over the world."

"Will you go back to Ireland to build them?"

He shook his head firmly. "I'll never go back. Me family is all but gone now, and the prospects of work are slim."

"Will you stay here?"

"I'll stay only as long as there's work." He opened his eyes wide and sat up. "I'm afraid to say, miss," he said, looking suddenly sad, "that on our last trip we also purchased a new canal boat. It's in harbor in Burlington, still. We'll be taking it through the locks to the Hudson." He paused and gazed down at his hands. "Leaving in a few days' time. There's no saying when I'll be back." I was stunned at his words, and could not find my way to a proper reply. Farley's visits were unpredictable, but I had begun to rely on him. He was the one person I really knew. The only one who knew me.

"I'm sorry, miss. I am, truly. I would have liked to stay." We sat for a long time before he spoke again.

"And what about yourself, miss? What do you wish for? To be a grand lady with a palace and land to spare?"

"Maybe." I couldn't imagine myself staying at the Manor without the prospect of Farley's visits.

"Cheer up, miss. Let's enjoy the time we have. Let's see a smile on your face." But I could not muster a smile.

"Come, now. What do you see for yourself?"

I shrugged. "I don't know. I guess I'd just like to go outside one day and not fear the wind."

He smiled. "Then today is your day." He stood and picked up the old ball of twine the Hounds had dragged with them and abandoned. Then he took off his leather belt and folded the waist of his pants over twice to keep them up. He unwound the twine, measuring it against the length of his forearm. When he had the right length, he took out his pocket knife and cut it.

"The Hounds won't like it."

"Blast the Hounds. They'll never know. Come here, then, miss."

"What?"

"Come on, now. No fear." I stood up, shook the sand from my clothes and walked over to him.

"Now, put the belt around your waist." I did as he instructed. He took the twine and double- and triple-knotted it around the belt's buckle, not a weaver's knot, but the hard, fast knot of a fisherman.

"Now take off your boots."

"I can't."

"Why not?"

"If I do, I might get picked up."

"That's the point, miss."

"Oh, no. Please, Farley. You don't understand. It's frightening being picked up."

"But to be a great lady, you can't fear the wind. What if you have to go out to survey your lands and check to make sure the peasants are well fed? Will you be forever holed up in your palace?" I laughed. "Besides, it'll be different this time. You won't get taken. I'm here and I'll hold firm. Do you trust that I'll hold you?"

"Yes. I do trust you, of course." And I meant it. Farley was the person I trusted the most, though I had known him such a short time. He didn't think me strange for my size or tease me for my fear. He understood something about me that not even I understood.

"Well then?" I looked down at my heavy boots and Farley's bare feet and I longed to feel the sand against my soles. "You'll have to leave them behind."

"Yes, but I cannot promise what will happen, even whether I'll be taken. The wind is unpredictable."

I bent down and began unlacing my boots. When they were free, I tossed them onto the beach and dug my toes into the sand, the way any other person might. Perhaps I had once, as a small child, felt this sensation, but I could not remember. For me, it was entirely new, like tasting a sweet fruit for the very first time. The sand's warm grains caressed the bottoms of my feet. I longed to stand in it forever, but Farley was impatient.

"Come on now," he urged. "The wind is picking up. Take off your coat." I slid out of my coat and dropped it on the blanket. I took Wysteria's key ring and placed it beside the coat, feeling lighter than I had in a long time.

"What should I do?"

"Run. Run like we do with the kites. Make believe you're the Dragon and I'm holding your line." The line was long enough for me to run ten or twelve yards down the beach away from him. I'm sure it must have looked ridiculous, Farley holding on to me with a ball of twine, but I did as he said.

"When you feel yourself starting to lift off, yank on the line so I'll know."

"You'll know," I yelled over the wind. It did not take long. A gust swept under me and I was suddenly airborne. I yanked at the line, but by then it was obvious that my feet were no longer on the sand. Farley braced himself, wedging his legs between two large boulders near our blanket.

"Will you look at yourself!" I heard him exclaim.

I cannot fully describe the feeling of being lifted off the ground—I can only say it makes your stomach jump and something in your chest squeeze tightly about your heart. I waited for the moment when I would tumble out of control, be sent hurtling into a tree or against the cliffs. I braced for impact, but it did not come. Surprised, I lifted my head into the wind and saw only the open sky before me. Slowly, I put my arms out to my sides and glided above the beach, above the rocks and the gulls digging for clams, and above Farley, who stared up at me not in fear or disapproval, but in amazement. I could feel his strength on the other end of the line. I was airborne, and for the first time that I could remember, I was not afraid. As I soared above the earth, a sure and certain knowing swept over me that with Farley as my anchor, I could lean into the wind and it would carry me.

Farley was trying to tell me something, but I could not hear his words over the rush of the wind.

He mimed his request by holding his free arm out and tilting it at an angle. I nodded and tilted my own arms to the right and then to the left and the wind obeyed my commands and sent me in first one direction and then the other. Farley cheered.

There was no one to see me, no eyes upon me but Farley's. All fear slipped away. I felt as free as a gliding hawk or an eagle. The wind filled all the space around me, so that I could hear nothing but its voice. I could move only as far as the line would allow, but with my newfound ability to guide myself, I soared over the whole range of beach where Farley and I had spent our days, seeing it all from a new perspective. I tried to find the spot where I thought the mysterious fire had been, but there was no evidence of it that I could see. I looked upon the Manor, dark and foreboding, perched precariously upon the cliffs, and I realized that no matter how bleak its facade, how dark its interior, neither the Manor nor Wysteria could ever truly threaten me. In their shadow, I had simply forgotten who I was. I had wrongly put my security in the hands of a house, a structure made of wood and nails, and of a woman who did not know my true nature. I was a creature of the air. This I knew now with certainty. I was not bound to any substance of earth, including that forbidding dwelling upon the cliff. I must always stay close to the wind, I told myself, as I caught an updraft and soared ever higher, pulling tightly on the line. No matter what happened, I must always stay within its embrace.

I could see the gulls, not unlike me, catching the currents and gliding at eye level. And I could see below me the Hounds, worried and confused, racing down the beach toward Farley, barking at the spectacle of my figure in the air.

Farley saw them, too, and quickly brought in the line, drawing me back to earth. I landed a bit roughly, but I was safe and intact and quickly surrounded, pushed into the sand by the Hounds' giant, inquisitive paws and wet tongues. Farley rushed over and freed me.

"Off with you, beasts," he laughed, pushing the Hounds aside. He regally bent over and extended his hand, gazing at me with quiet admiration.

"Your first flight, miss."

12

I awoke to a world of wind and sand, the smell of fresh air and dampness, a lingering memory of flight.

I was not in my own bed, or in the captain's study, but bundled in a blanket on the beach close to a smoldering fire.

Farley and I had spent the whole glorious day at the lakeside, and when the sun began to set, I could not bear to think of returning to the oppressive walls of the Manor. At Farley's suggestion, we built a fire and fell asleep talking of the wings.

I had so desperately wanted to tell him of the uneasy feeling that each day grew larger within me, of the sense that I could almost put my finger upon the whole truth of the Manor, the fortune, and the captain's death, only to find that the closer I came, the more quickly it scurried away and eluded me. I had hoped that with his help, in the open air away from the Manor, I could make sense of the puzzling stories that swirled within me, but I found I could not. For, more than I desired to lighten my own burden, I wished not to entangle Farley in the Manor's web of lies.

"It's morning, miss," Farley said, shaking me fully awake. "Will you see to the Hounds?" Though we had secured the kites before falling asleep, the Hounds had been given their freedom and were now somewhere above the cliffs, barking and creating a ruckus.

"Yes, I'll see to them." I brushed the sand from my face, stood up and untied the twine from around my waist. I had slept in my coat and boots. As well, Farley had secured me fast to one of the boulders so I would not blow away in the night.

"You'll be back soon?" he asked.

"Of course. I'll feed the Hounds and bring us some breakfast. When I return, will we work on the wings again?"

Farley smiled. "Indeed we will. Perhaps today I can make sense of them."

I ran to the top of the cliffs, my heart lightened by the promise of spending another day in the open air with Farley. All thoughts of his departure and the dilemma I faced temporarily faded from my mind and were replaced by the hope that today we might come closer to unraveling the mystery of the kites.

I found the Hounds, barking not at a rabbit or squirrel as I had suspected, but at Dr. Mead, who stood at the entrance to the Manor, keeping his distance from their strong jaws.

"So you are here," he said, clearly relieved. He looked as if he had not slept well in many nights. Dark circles ringed his eyes, and his usually well-groomed hair was swept about by the wind. "I did not see the lantern last night and grew concerned for your welfare."

The lantern. I had forgotten entirely about lighting it. "I'm sorry to have caused you worry, Doctor. It was such a lovely evening that I built a fire on the beach and fell asleep beside it. I have only just now woken." I felt more guarded in my speech than I had been with Dr. Mead on his previous visits. I kept looking into his eyes for some clue as to his intentions, but he appeared only tired and distracted. Still, the nurse's words would not leave me. *I do not know what he realizes, nor what he covets. . . .*

"Then you are fine?"

"Yes, sir, I am fine. The weather has broken and I

was drawn outside to the fresh air, that is all." I did not wish to divulge Farley's presence. Dr. Mead might find it improper and forbid me to stay on my own.

He nodded, eyeing me with curiosity. "I have come with news. You are not to remain alone much longer. Mrs. Barrows is on the mend. She requires little more attention at St. Elias's and wishes to return here."

"When, sir?"

"Two days hence. I will bring her myself in the evening."

"Two days?" I could not keep the shock from my voice.

"Do these arrangements not please you?"

How could I tell him that no arrangements would please me, except that I stay with Farley? In the month of Wysteria's absence, my life had changed. I had a friend, the first in my life. I could take to the wind with his help and see a future apart from the Manor. I knew that I could not remain on my own forever, but I also could not see myself living with Wysteria, for I found that my trust in her was rapidly waning.

"Does this not please you?" the doctor repeated.

"No. I am, of course, greatly pleased by Wysteria's

recovery. I just . . ." I reached into my pocket and rolled the small glass bottle worriedly against my palm.

"What is it you have there?" Dr. Mead inquired, gesturing to my pocket.

I hesitated. I had suspected that the writing on the bottle might be his, but I was not certain. Perhaps all doctors wrote in a similar hand. Yet if anyone might be able to explain its contents to me, it would be Dr. Mead. I pulled it from my pocket and handed it to him.

The doctor removed his glasses and held the bottle up to the light.

"Laudanum," he whispered, reading the scrawl with no effort.

"What is laudanum, sir?"

The doctor's face flushed. He appeared suddenly alarmed, as if the bottle in his hand contained some terrible memory he wished to expunge, but then he quickly cleared his throat and composed himself.

"A sedative. Not harmful when used in its proper dosage. Where did you find this?"

"In Wysteria's bedchamber. I was looking for her keys when I came upon it. There were more bottles. All empty, with the exception of this one."

The doctor sighed.

"Why would she have this, sir?"

"I prescribed this for the captain many years ago, at Mrs. Barrows's request. She was concerned that her husband was not sleeping well, so I encouraged her to give him this tincture in small doses. Apparently she used it for purposes other than for what it was intended."

"Why would my name be on this bottle?"

"I do not know. Several more bottles, you say? Do they look as if they've been there a long time?"

"Yes, sir. But for this one, all were covered in dust."

Dr. Mead held the bottle tightly in his hand and walked to the cliff's edge. He ran his fingers through his hair. I thought for a moment he might cast the bottle out into the lake, but he did not. Instead he turned to me.

"You need not fear, young lady. Mrs. Barrows will receive no more bottles of laudanum or anything else from me." He slipped it into his pocket.

"Thank you, sir."

"Now, I must ask you a favor before I depart."

I cringed, for I knew what this favor was and I did not wish to grant it.

"As I mentioned to you, the captain once told me of a secret within the Manor, and I have spent these many years wondering if indeed there was such a thing. The last few nights, I have pondered where it might be. If I might have one more opportunity to look about the captain's study before Mrs. Barrows returns, I may very well discover it."

"Do you think it wise, sir?" Honoring Miss Moreland's plea to refuse him entrance seemed the best recourse, yet I knew, from the urgency of his manner, that the only answer he would accept from me would be yes.

"I ask only for a few moments of your time."

Though I was apprehensive, I felt I had no choice and so agreed and led the doctor into the Manor and up to the captain's study. I let the Hounds in with us but bade them stay on the main floor. Once inside the study, I closed the door and walked immediately over to the window, where I could see Farley on the beach below. Just to be safe, I stood with my back to the window to prevent the doctor from detecting Farley's presence, but I need not have feared, for the moment the doctor entered the room, his focus became singular, and he began systematically searching through drawers and cupboards. I watched him grow more and more agitated as he failed to uncover what he sought, and an intense fear came over me, especially as he neared the bookcase. What if he pressed heavily upon it and found the entrance to the attic? There was nothing left inside it but some bolts of silk, the paper-making device and an old mortar and pestle, yet I could not shake the ever-increasing sense of dread that seemed to be filling the room as his search became more furious.

"I cannot understand where it could be," he mumbled to himself.

"I know that Wysteria had the Manor thoroughly searched after the captain's death," I volunteered, "but no trace of a treasure was found, if that is what you seek." He seemed not to hear my words but continued speaking, and as he did so, riffled through the maps and papers on the captain's desk.

"The captain was a creative genius. His mind did not work like that of ordinary men. He took pleasure in riddles and complicated outcomes."

"I'm sorry, but I do not know how to help you, sir."

"Don't you?" The doctor suddenly turned on me. "A smart girl like you? You must know more than you are telling. You must have a secret that you will not confide." I shook my head, taken aback by his sudden anger.

"Tell me, or by God I'll shake it out of you." The doctor lunged forward, grabbing me violently by the shoulders, almost lifting me off the ground. My legs began to tremble and I felt myself on the verge of crying, but I could not allow it. I must remain calm. The Manor had surely taken hold of the doctor, as Miss Moreland had predicted, for he was now clearly out of his head.

"No, sir. I promise you," I said, my voice shaking. "I harbor no secrets to help you in your quest. There is nothing I know of in this room of any value." Even as I uttered these words I began to fear that what the doctor wanted was somehow connected to the kites, though what value they would hold for him, I did not know.

He gripped me more tightly. I wanted to scream for Farley, but I knew he could not hear me.

"You meddlesome child. Why do you stand in the way of what is due me? Why must there always be something in the way? I wish only to claim what is rightfully mine and once belonged to my family." He grasped me ever more tightly.

"Please, sir, you're hurting me!" At that moment, there was a bump against the door and the doctor immediately released his hold. In my fright, I sank to the floor, my legs no longer able to bear my weight.

"Are we not alone in this house?" he asked, a look of terror flashing across his face. I could see that the stories of the Manor had pervaded his imagination and he believed it possible that a spirit now lay on the other side of the door.

I could not speak but found the strength to rise to my knees, reach over and quickly free the latch before the doctor could stop me.

On the threshold stood the Hounds, all four of them, the fur on their necks straight along their spines. A low growl began to emerge from the throat of one, and the others followed suit.

The doctor froze in fear. I recovered my courage, stood and walked to the doorway, securing my position amid my guardians. I did not stop them from growling, but held my hand out to keep them still.

"I do not know what came over me . . . ," the doctor said, running his hand through his hair. "I apologize, young lady. I must . . ."

"You must leave the Manor, sir," I said firmly, stepping aside. "I fear it has a bad effect upon you."

"Yes. Yes, you are right, of course." The Hounds and I followed him downstairs. I had seen with my own eyes the Manor's pull upon the doctor and did not trust him to be free of its menace until he was safely outside its doors. I wished him to leave as soon as possible.

"It is time for you to be on your way, Dr. Mead. Your horse is waiting at the gate." I pointed it out to

him. He seemed dazed and exhausted, yet he followed my advice without delay.

"Thank you," he said. He began walking away,
then turned.

"Shall I expect the light tonight?"

"Yes, Dr. Mead. Tonight and tomorrow as well."

"I . . ." But his words fell away from him.

"Good day, Dr. Mead."

I made sure the doctor's horse had rounded the bend,
and the Hounds had returned to the beach, before I
went back inside the Manor. I headed directly to the
captain's study, for there was something I desperately
needed to know. I pulled out a heavy leather-bound
dictionary from the captain's bookshelf and looked up

> *laudanum: powdered opium mixed with equal
> parts alcohol and water, often sweetened. Some-
> times known as wine of opium. Painkiller and
> sedative. Given in extreme doses can lead to hallu-
> cination and death.*

Had Wysteria given the captain the laudanum to
make him docile and forget about selling the Manor,
or had she given him too much, as the doctor implied,
causing him to go mad, to hallucinate, to perhaps

think he could fly? Dr. Mead had prescribed the laudanum to the captain but I knew he had not intended it to be misused. Miss Moreland had been right. The doctor was not a bad man, only susceptible to the Manor, as so many others had been.

I closed the book. But what of the bottle reserved for me? Did Wysteria anticipate that one day I, too, would challenge her authority or ask too many questions? Did she intend to keep me docile or do away with me, as she had her husband? For I felt with certainty that she was capable of doing so. I knew enough now. I had to heed Miss Moreland's words and leave as soon as I was able. Dr. Mead could no longer manage himself in regard to the Manor. Any trust I had placed in him was now gone.

My only hope lay with Farley and the wings. We had two days. Surely in that time Farley would understand how to build them. Surely we would find a way, for my situation had grown dire. I must leave the Manor before Wysteria returned. I must go far away. Very far away.

If indeed the captain was a creative genius, a man of riddles, as the doctor had said, he must have had a plan for the kites. If nothing else, he would not have left without documenting his ideas. He had made detailed notes about the intricate underpinnings of his vessels. Surely he would have left behind some sketch or diagram, though I had never come upon any rendering in his records. The attic, too, was entirely devoted to the kites; there was neither a desk there nor documents of any kind.

Suddenly, a vivid image of the captain as a young boy came to my mind. I had never thought of the captain in this way before, but, of course, he had once been the same age as me. He had grown up in Bourne Manor, as I had. Alone, as I had. His days had been spent, I was sure, in much the same ways as my own. He was a clever boy and imaginative. The doctor had described him as a dreamer and unlike ordinary men.

In a house of moving walls and secret passages, of rooms filled with kites and skeleton keys, was it not possible that he had written his ideas in some sort of code or hidden them, as a young boy might? Hidden them first from his family and then from Wysteria, believing that perhaps both would have destroyed his hopes and belittled his vision?

Where would a boy hide something of value? I opened drawers, pulled books from their shelves, searched for secret compartments in the floorboards, but to no avail.

I sat down in the captain's chair at his desk and

stared at the walls of his study, until it occurred to me that I was staring at the very answer itself. The small pieces of paper wedged into the cracks beneath the window casements! Those seemingly useless scraps of yellowing parchment I had taken to be Wysteria's primitive form of insulation against the cold.

I stood up and walked to the window, knelt down and pried one carefully from its crevice. It was tightly wound like a miniature scroll. I unrolled it gently, for it was amazingly fragile. It was made from the same type of paper as the kites. Written upon it were calculations of some kind. I pried out another, which revealed a tiny sketch of a pair of wings.

I pulled out several more scrolls and unrolled these as well. Upon each were various renditions of a man with wings strapped to his shoulders, standing on a mountaintop. Some sketches were clearly done by the hand of a child and were so old they almost disintegrated at my touch. Others were newer, finely drawn, with streams of notes written around them. There were, too, long entries of dates and weather predictions. I pulled out all the scrolls I could find, more than fifty in all, gently placed them in the pockets of my coat and hurried downstairs.

I packed apples, a bag of dried plums and a piece of meat from the larder, enough for two days. I stuffed all of it into a net bag and slung it over my shoulder. I walked to the front door and reached for the large brass knob, turning it with my free hand, but could not grasp it. I tried then with my other hand but found the door firmly locked. I could not remember locking it behind me. I took out key after key, but none would work. With each key, the door remained locked. I next tried the windows, but they too refused to open. I could feel fear quickly rising within me, threatening to take hold.

I ran up the stairs, trying every door and every window, but all refused to give way. For one brief, terrible moment, I imagined that I would be trapped inside the Manor forever, with the knowledge of my freedom stuffed in my coat pockets. But to my immense relief, this hopeless image faded as I pushed my way into the glass room, which had no lock upon it, and out onto the widow's walk.

Far below me on the beach, I could see Farley and the Hounds, though they could not see or hear me. In my panic, I thought to leap the impossible gap to the elm tree, a good two yards, but fortunately I quickly came to my senses and realized that I could, with the help of the anchor line, make my way down the side of the house.

I tied the net bag tightly at the top and dropped it

down the four stories to the ground. Returning to the glass room, I lit the lantern, putting it on low and filling its reservoir with oil, enough to last two days, to allay any suspicions on the doctor's part. I then took up the anchor line and tied it about my waist. It was long and it was strong and able to hold my weight. I secured the other end of the line to the railing, climbed over and slowly let myself down the side of the Manor, being careful not to let the tiny scrolls leave my pockets.

I could go only as far as the rope hung, but at that point I was close enough to jump without fear of injury. Firmly on the ground, I grabbed the net bag and looked up at the Manor. Its vacant and menacing windows glared down upon me, and I knew, perhaps for the first time, its real intentions. It would try to destroy me before it ever let me go. I knew with certainty that this was true, and I vowed that never again would I be caught inside its walls.

13

Our time of freedom was drawing to a close. Dr. Mead would return with Wysteria in two days. Farley and I pored over the captain's scrolls, a cryptic yet revealing account of Lawrence Barrows's life that included detailed sketches of his amazing creation, the Flying Heron.

As a boy, Lawrence Barrows had been fascinated with birds and flight. He had designed kites and flown them on the beach. He later dreamed of a life at sea and voyages to places far away from his desolate boyhood home. He signed on to a merchant sailing vessel and traveled to Burma and the islands of Indonesia, where he heard for the first time the ancient stories of man-bearing kites. He collected fine silk fabric and bamboo and brought them home to reconstruct the creations that had captured his imagination. He studied the wind, the motion of birds and the art of papermaking. Though there was no evidence that he planned to fly away himself, it was clear that he found great joy in his kites, for they could do the thing that he could not.

It was all there in the scrolls: his sketches of herons and ospreys, his desire to leave the Manor with Wysteria and set himself and Dr. Mead free at last from the Manor's curse.

"I still do not understand what fortune Dr. Mead thinks the captain left him," I said to Farley, for I had told him of Dr. Mead's alarming behavior.

"It must be something that one does not directly see when looking at it, like the wings. It must require a different kind of seeing."

"The doctor accused me of hiding a secret, and I thought perhaps the kites were the thing of great value that he sought, but what possible value could the kites have for a man like Dr. Mead? Their only value was to the captain, who simply loved to build them, and to me."

"Perhaps the silk kites are valuable. Perhaps the silk is rare."

"But there are not that many silk kites and only a few bolts of silk. The rest are all paper."

"Yes. The paper kites. They were made with great care."

"And they are unusual, but I do not think—"

"The paper!" Farley said suddenly. "The captain made his own paper, did he not?"

"Yes. But paper is of no great value."

Farley picked up one of the paper kites and held it in the sunlight, studying it closely. He smiled, then laughed and began dancing around with the kite in his hands.

"Farley? What is it?"

"Your captain was not only an excellent maker of kites, but a genius as well. Though perhaps a little eccentric, indeed."

"Farley!"

"This paper has always seemed familiar to me and yet strange. It is not what it seems."

"It is just paper."

"It is paper money, miss. Paper bills. These kites are made of hundreds or thousands of bills, perhaps some of large denominations, reconstituted and refined to make this exquisite paper. Here. See for yourself." I held the kite close and Farley pointed out to me the particular grain, the distinctive fibers, the now unmistakably green hue and the texture.

"The fortune is in the kites!" I exclaimed.

"Yes. It was a noble act. He knew a fortune would only bring further suffering upon his wife and friend, for the captain was a true friend."

"Unlike Dr. Mead, who searches for something that does not exist."

"It is only of value to you. It has fallen into the hands of the one person who truly knows how to use it."

Farley and I talked for a long time about the paper fortune. We talked of the wings and diligently studied the captain's scrolls, for we both knew that we must understand his plans for the Heron if I were to make my escape in time.

Interpreting the captain's notes, Farley explained to me that to cross the distance to the mountains, one had to replicate the actions of a bird by catching the warm thermal updrafts above the earth, then letting these drafts spin one up and out across the lake. The flier must also launch from the greatest height possible, which the captain identified as the roof of the glass house, a space of two yards with no railing about it, enough for three or four large steps.

"This clearly will be your way out, miss. Me boat is leaving tomorrow and if I am not on it, I will have forfeited a stable livelihood. You cannot be here when your mistress returns, and you cannot come with me.

I will help you to launch the Heron and I will watch you sail over the lake to the other side."

"But I do not know how to operate the wings. I will not know which strings to pull, or how to negotiate the currents and thermals of which you speak."

"We will practice until you do. Until you feel strong with the levers and the pulleys. You are a natural creature of the air, miss, and the wind draws you where it wants you. All you must do is let it take you to your destination. It will feel as natural to you as it would to any bird."

I knew Farley was right. There was no other way for me.

"Your only chance is to fly across the lake in hopes that you will find more of your own kind."

I nodded.

"We have much in our favor, miss," he said to encourage me. "We are nearing the end of June and there are warmer currents. You will glide over the mowed fields to the north and then ride the thermals out over the water. You are as light as a feather and easily lifted by the wind."

We spent the remainder of that day and the next following the captain's directions for the Heron. We had all the pieces required, except for a few wooden braces, which Farley carved out of driftwood and attached with twine. Although it first appeared complex, Farley showed me that the design for the Heron was in reality quite simple. Seven kites fastened perfectly together made up one wing, and two wings connected to a braided harness. A hinge at midwing bent at the pull of a cord to allow it to flap. Farley demonstrated it to me, showing how, if kept at a constant rhythm, the wings, in fact, replicated the motion of a heron's. There were, as well, intricate and subtle curves and details built into the design of the kites that mimicked the exact arch of a bird's wing, a tail that tilted upward and the ability to collapse the giant wings in order to carry them.

"I am surprised that we could not see it earlier," Farley remarked. "If we had only turned the kites over to fit them as if into a puzzle, we could have known its rightful shape."

Farley altered the apparatus as best he could to fit my small frame, but it sagged at my shoulders, and I was so light that when we practiced working with it along the beach, it tilted and threw me into a somersault, almost crushing the wings. Still, I was determined to succeed, for I knew that I had no other choice.

The apparatus fit Farley well enough and he was sufficiently heavy to stabilize it, but that did us little good. We practiced adding weight to my pockets and tying the straps down tighter, but still the wings were unwieldy.

"I will have to adjust it once again," Farley said, taking the wings from my back.

"We don't have much time," I reminded him. "Dr. Mead will return with Wysteria tomorrow."

"Yes, I know." Farley sat by the fire and began restringing the harness. All day, I had felt that a heavy decision lay upon his mind, though he would not speak of it. As the light began to fade and every possible angle had been considered to fit the harness to me, Farley quietly unlaced it and laid it on the ground. Then the burden suddenly seemed to lift from him and his eyes lit up. The Hounds came up to him and licked his face. He did not push them away, as he had in the past. Deep in thought, he hardly noticed them. Absentmindedly he put his arm around one of their giant heads and smiled.

"I know," he said. "I know what I must do. Do not worry, miss. We will find a way."

14

The day of the flight dawned overcast with the threat of rain, but by noon the sky had cleared and promised to remain bright.

Farley left shortly after breakfast. He said he had important matters to see to in town and would return by early evening.

"I will be as quick as I can. The wind will be best after sunset. We'll launch then." I nodded, hoping that he would return before Wysteria did.

"You must promise me that you will not go inside the Manor. While I am gone you will stay here on the beach far away from its doors. Promise me?"

"I promise. I do not wish to go near it."

"That may not be possible, for we will have to make our way to the top of the house to launch the Heron."

"I cannot face it."

"We will face it together. You will by no means venture near the Manor alone until I return?" I assured him again that I would not.

With that, Farley departed. The Hounds left for a morning of roaming, and I stayed on the beach, occupying myself by cutting several pieces of twine and weaving them into six strong cords. Farley assured me we would need these during the launch, though I did not know their purpose.

As the afternoon wore on and my weaving was almost complete, my thoughts began to wander to the Manor: my fear of it, the captain's desire to be rid of it, and how Dr. Mead and Wysteria, too, had been taken fully under its spell. I could see quite clearly how all of us and generations of Barrowses and Meads had been bound to it in an inexplicable way, as had the spirits of all that still dwelt there.

Looking up at its looming silhouette, I felt a strange sympathy for the Manor. It had not asked to be built upon the cliffs, nor had it anything to do with its crooked design. It had been a victim of circumstance. It suffered from the isolation of its placement, as did its inhabitants. From the distance of the beach, I could see that it was only a house. It had taken me in. Surely I must not repay it by leaving in this way. Surely I should show my respect and bid it a proper farewell.

In the light of day, the Manor appeared almost harmless, and I found my pity for it growing with each passing minute. I was pulled toward it not only in thought, but also physically, and I wanted nothing more than to be once again within its protective embrace. My resolution to stay close to the wind faded from my mind. Something drew me beyond my normal senses. Though I knew I should not even let myself think of the Manor, I found that I could think of nothing else. The Manor needed me, I was sure of it. It would cease to exist if I did not return to the safety of its walls.

Memories of my days within its many rooms, looking out the windows and standing on the walk, filled my mind. Nostalgia overtook me and, like a strong perfume, drew me ever closer, until I found myself standing before the gates leading to the entrance. Mesmerized, I started for the front door, ready to lose myself inside, when a flock of starlings alighted from a nearby ash tree and awoke me from my stupor. I heard quite distinctly in the flapping of their wings Farley's voice, which was stronger even than the pull of the Manor.

"We will face it together," the voice said. And

with that, I snapped fully awake, as if rescued from a very bad dream, and could not imagine how I had come to stand so close to the Manor's doors. The Hounds appeared at my side and gently guided me back to the beach, where I remained, watching the sun sink behind the mountains, turning the sky orange and crimson until all color eventually faded, leaving the horizon the deep azure of the lake itself at twilight.

I added wood to the fire and made the final adjustments to the cords I had completed. The Hounds settled in beside me, their gangly legs occasionally getting caught up in the harness strings, requiring me to free them. They stayed close, and whenever a thought of the Manor came to me I called them to my side. I dismissed all thoughts of the Manor with a firm, audible "No," until the thoughts began to fade and lose their hold on me.

Farley was true to his word and at eight o'clock returned, carrying a satchel on his back.

"Were you fine, then?" he asked.

"Yes," I said.

"I worried."

"No need."

"Come, now. We cannot delay. The wind is right." Together we picked up the Heron, collapsed it, and carried it to the top of the cliffs. The Hounds tried to follow us, but Farley pushed them away from the fragile wings.

"Miss, please keep them at bay. They will destroy all of our hard work."

I called the Hounds to my side and knew what I must tell them. I knelt down to look into their giant faces. They were huge and smelly and wild, but they had been my protectors, even before I knew I needed their protection.

"You must listen to me now," I said, gathering them around me. "It is time for us to leave this place. When Wysteria returns tonight, you need to be very far away. Do you understand?" They cocked their heads. "You must leave when I leave. You no longer need a mistress to govern you. You are free, as I am." One Hound began to whine, and the rest joined in. "Hush! Look there," I said, pointing across the lake to the mountains. "That is where I am going. That is where you will find me. You can find me. I know you can."

"Miss. Come along!" Farley called.

"I'm coming," I said.

"You must stay outside," I said to the Hounds. They whimpered and sat on their haunches. I bent down and kissed the top of each of their heads, then turned away from their sorrowful faces. I ran to catch up with Farley, trying not to weep, for I had grown to love the beasts and hoped with all my heart that they would find me.

Together, Farley and I slowly approached the Manor and pushed open the massive front door. All was quiet and dark within. I had forgotten how deep the gloom was inside the house at that time of the day with the heavy curtains drawn over the windows.

"Farley," I whispered.

"Hold me hand," he said calmly. I took hold. How strange that he had no fear of the place at all and that my own legs shook so badly I could barely stand upon them.

"It is not real," he whispered. "This place is only a thought that has grabbed hold of you. It cannot harm you. You are not of this place, and it has no power over you. You do not need it, nor do you owe it your allegiance." I nodded, listening only to his words and not to the rattling of the windows, which had begun as soon as we had stepped inside.

"Pull back the draperies," Farley whispered. We carefully placed the Heron on the floor. He took one side of the great room and I took the other, and silently we pulled the heavy drapes back from the frames, though the windows shook and groaned in their casements.

"Now open the windows," he said.

"They're locked," I whispered back.

"Take the keys and open them."

"I'm not sure they will work."

"Try." I fumbled with the keys, trying to remember which one opened the windows. *"Long and thin,"* I murmured, *"long and thin."* My hands shook with fear, but finally I found the right key and freed each window. Against their rattling, Farley and I pushed them open wide.

"Open all the doors," Farley said then.

"No!"

"Yes. We'll open all the doors and move quickly to the next floor and do the same there," he insisted.

"But what if it won't let us?"

"The house senses your fear and plays upon it. That is the only thing that will stop us. When the fear presses upon you, remember that it is not real. Remember the feeling of the wind. That is real."

I nodded, for I knew this to be true. I held my thoughts firm, and, keeping the Heron from catching beneath our feet, we moved to the next floor.

Along the staircase, I passed the portraits of the captain and his ancestors, all those who had not escaped the ravages of the Manor, all those who had been ruled by something they could not see. And I knew in that moment that I would not be like them.

"Trust me?"

"I do."

"Go." I knew which keys opened the doors on each floor and quickly released them, running up stairs and down corridors until all the doors and windows were free and Farley and I were safely inside the glass house.

Farley prepared the Heron, spreading its wings wide on the floor and adjusting the harness.

"How will you get out?" I asked him. "Once I'm gone, how will you leave? By the tree?"

"Don't worry yourself about that," he said, winking at me.

All the doors open now, the house began to shake furiously. Floorboards groaned beneath us as an enormous wave of turmoil and grief rose up from its depths. But the more the Manor raged, the more I held to Farley's words that it was not real and that it could not harm me.

"We don't have much time," Farley said. I followed him out to the walk and began to strap on the harness, but he stopped me and shook his head.

"*I* will wear the wings," he announced. "They fit me and I can operate them." He took them gently from me and spread them open again. "Hand me the cords you made." I did as he asked, and he secured himself to the frame.

"I don't understand. What will *I* do?"

"You, miss," he said, putting his hand on my shoulder, "are a friend of the wind. You will hold me hand."

"You're coming with me?"

He pointed to his satchel. "All me belongings are inside. I'll be taking me freedom, as you are. I have all me wages and we have a plan, do we not?"

I smiled. "We do."

"Come, now. We can talk of it later." Farley put the wings on, stood up on the railing and began climbing to the roof. "Take off your boots and when I am settled, you come up," he instructed.

I unlaced my boots and took them off, leaving them forever at the top of the Manor. I filled the lantern one last time and lit the wick, for it had burned down and the light was barely visible. I did not wish for Dr. Mead to suspect anything, though I knew he would soon enough when he arrived with Wysteria and only my boots were to be found.

"Now!" Farley yelled. I climbed up on the railing as I had seen him do and onto the roof, which was sturdy, but not broad. The two of us barely fit upon it.

"Wait," I said. In my haste, I had forgotten to

close the door to the glass house, and the lantern stood vulnerable and exposed to the wind. "I must see to the lantern. The wind is strong."

"There is no time," Farley said. "Leave it." As he spoke, we heard a rumbling rise from within the house and the whole structure swayed violently toward the lake. A strong gust whipped about us, and as I grabbed Farley's arm, we heard the definite crash of the lantern as the wind knocked it to the floor. After all my years as its keeper, on this day of all days, I could not believe that I had abandoned my post.

"Farley, please!"

"Give me your hand!" he yelled.

"Please. The house will burn! It will burn to the ground."

"We cannot go back! Your hand! Give me your hand!" I thought of the Manor beneath us and of all that would be destroyed if I did not see to the lantern, all that would be lost. But then I looked up at Farley, at his hand reaching for mine, and I grabbed it, my heart beating in my throat. Before I could catch my breath or think another thought, Farley pulled the harness strings tight, the wings opened and we ran together off the roof, gliding out over the great elm, heading north above the fields until the warm currents buoyed us high enough and pushed us toward the lake. The wind lifted under the Heron's wings, and beneath my frame, carrying me along as naturally as any bird. I leaned into it, giving myself completely to its embrace.

"Don't look back," Farley yelled. But of all the things he had asked of me, this was the one thing I could not do. I was unable to take my eyes from the Manor as it was slowly consumed, the flames spreading first to the roof and then working down to the third-floor balconies, the turrets and the tower that held my room, taking the captain's study along with them.

Far out on the plains, I could see a carriage hurrying down the road to the Manor. Nearing the front gate, it pulled to a stop, and a tall, willowy figure in black descended the steps and ran headlong toward the burning structure. A man in a top hat and dark cape stepped out behind her, staring at the blaze before him. Just as I was about to turn away, I saw him lift his eyes to the sky and fix his gaze upon the Heron.

High on the cliffs, the Hounds raced northward after us, howling wildly, their long strides carrying them safely away from the destruction.

"Run! I whispered. "Run until you find us."

As the wind pushed us across the lake, I heard a

faint but definite roar as the Manor collapsed upon itself. In our wake, the entire hillside above the cliffs was awash in light. And far below, on the crimson sand, I saw, to my surprise, a distinct but smaller fire extinguishing itself on the beach.

15

As all things of the world are meant to pass on and be no more, so Bourne Manor disappeared from the shores of Lake Champlain, letting loose its grip on the red stone cliffs, on Wysteria Barrows, and myself. Freed from its own bondage, Bourne Manor's light blazed one last time over the lake, sending a fierce warning to all sailors and fishermen to heed the dangerous rocks that guarded the entrance to its harbor—calling no more lost souls to its ominous doors.

If such places as Bourne Manor carry within them the stories of a mournful past, as some believe, or harbor those lost unto themselves, then perhaps the Manor did indeed know more of me than I knew myself. Perhaps it knew that I would uncover the secret held within its walls in a set of wings crafted by a dreamer. Perhaps it foresaw the future I would bring to it on that February morning and welcomed me all the same.

I cannot know the purpose of dwellings lonely and forgotten. I know only that in the arms of the wind, both Wysteria and the Manor lost their grip upon me and I feared them no more, no more than a starling would fear the temporary entrapment of a barn gate, knowing that its true nature is not bound to earth.

I flew over the lake that night, neither blown off course nor caught in the currents, but safe in the wake of the captain's wings and not far from the reach of Farley's hand.

By the light of a rising moon and with the promise of finding those like myself, we safely reached the western shore.

acknowledgments

The author would like to thank the Vermont Community Foundation, Marc Bregman, Howard Fisher, Michael Fisher, Tom Murphy, Tassos Pappas, Kate Pietschman and Françoise Bui for their support, encouragement and inspiration in the writing of this book.

about the author

Rita Murphy lives in Vermont with her husband and their son. Her previous novels are *Looking for Lucy Buick, Harmony, Black Angels,* and *Night Flying.*